A WILL WITHIN A WHEEL

Women Racers of the 1890s

WRITTEN AND ILLUSTRATED BY T.R. ORMOND

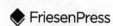 FriesenPress

One Printers Way
Altona, MB R0G 0B0
Canada

www.friesenpress.com

Copyright © 2024 by T.R. Ormond
First Edition — 2024

ISBN
978-1-03-918206-6 (Hardcover)
978-1-03-918205-9 (Paperback)
978-1-03-918207-3 (eBook)

1. FICTION, HISTORICAL

Distributed to the trade by The Ingram Book Company

Dedicated to my wife, daughters, and mother
The illustrations I dedicate to my late father

TABLE OF CONTENTS

LIST OF ILLUSTRATIONS

A NOTE ON NOTES, NAMES AND TRANSLATION

Notes: *A Will within a Wheel*, though a work of fiction, is the product of research. In order to ensure the reading experience is not impeded by endnotes, I have decided to forgo any formal system of citation. There is, however, a complete list of notes at the end of the book for those who wish to learn more about my sources.

Names: Chapter Three of this book takes place in Russia. It is perhaps worthwhile reminding readers about the customs around names in the Russian language. A person's name can take different forms. The level of familiarity between the speaker and the holder of the name determines the correct usage. So, for example, the Russian prince in my story is Prince Dmitri Alexandrovich Shirinskii-Shikhmatov. It would be polite and correct to address him as Dmitri Alexandrovich, or as Prince Shirinskii-Shikhmatov. I playfully have some characters address him as *"Mon Prince,"* but they are French and unfamiliar with Russian culture. Only someone in his most intimate circle would be able to call him simply Dmitri, and only his nanny or his brother would dare to call him Dima.

Translation: A final note needs to be made regarding translation. This work makes extensive use of French and Russian journalism. Fortunately, I am able to translate from these languages on my own. Any deficiencies in those translations are my responsibility.

INTRODUCTION

Women Racers of the 1890s and the Great Bicycle Craze

The bicycle as we know it today appeared in 1885 when the "Rover Safety" was introduced into the market. The design's attractiveness lay, as its name suggests, in its relative safety. There had been other machines prior to its creation, but they were either extremely dangerous, or cumbersome, or both: there was the heavy and ponderous boneshaker, the towering penny-farthing, and a whole slew of lumbering and clumsy quadricycles and tricycles. All it took was a chain and two wheels of the same diameter to sweep all those earlier models away. In fact, it proved to be such a good design that we have not significantly altered it in more than 130 years. But it didn't immediately resonate with consumers. It took until roughly 1893 before it became mainstream. Suddenly there were hundreds of new trademarks appearing all over Europe, America, Australia, New Zealand and Canada. The so-called bicycle craze of the 1890s had begun, and personal transportation changed forever.

Women embraced this new technology, and by doing so they grasped new freedoms and responsibilities. Suffragist Susan B. Anthony wrote a famous letter to *Sidepaths* magazine in 1898. It sets the stage perfectly:

> Bicycling has done more to emancipate women than any-
> thing else in the world... I stand and rejoice every time
> I see a woman ride on a wheel. It gives her a feeling of
> freedom, self-reliance, and independence. The moment
> she takes her seat she knows she can't get into harm while
> she is on her bicycle, and away she goes, the picture of
> free, untrammeled womanhood.

Anthony continues her letter with details: the bicycle reformed how women dressed, it sent them out into public space, it made them equal to men in mobility and pleasure, and, through involvement with activism, it taught them about the legislative process and preached "the necessity for woman suffrage," still not yet a reality. Elsewhere she calls the bicycle a "Freedom Machine." She was not alone in her enthusiasm. Frances E. Willard, the leader of the Women's Christian Temperance Union, had spent her life encouraging young women to expand their social horizons by acquiring new skills and altering expectations. She learned to ride the bicycle at 54, and, realizing how perfectly it fit into her agenda, she wrote a book about it, *A Wheel within a Wheel*: "She who succeeds in gaining mastery of the bicycle will gain the mastery of life," she exhorted. Anthony and Willard offer two of the more notable voices connecting women's emancipation and the bicycle in the late Victorian Era. There are many, many more instances of it, attesting to its thoroughness and depth. It is as well-established as it is well-documented.

But it is too simplistic to claim this transformation was universal. Not all women's lives changed, not all women rode bicycles, and, of the women whose lives did change thanks to the bicycle, not all of them experienced that change in the same way. Variety, rather than uniformity, characterizes the era: in fact, the main joy in researching these women is tracing the diverse range of goals they sought, and the multitude of meanings they created. Really, Anthony and Willard's comments were only applicable to white women of the American and European bourgeoisie, people who resembled them: they were other suffragists and temperance activists, as well as members of the leisure class, for whom the bicycle was primarily a

1. The San Jose Women's Cycling Club

fashion accessory. Their stories are stimulating and valuable for shedding light on this period. They will make the subject of a subsequent book, but they will not appear in this one.

Women Racers

This book is about women who raced. To them, Anthony and Willard's ideas were too timid and genteel. Competitors with great ambition, they did not settle for mere "untrammeled womanhood"; instead, they sought absolute personal sovereignty. They were great athletes, women like Tillie Anderson, Lisette, Dottie Farnsworth, Victorine Reillo, Rosina Lane, and Gabrielle Étéogella to name a few. There were many more. They were all exceptional people whose lives in no way resembled those of their mothers (or for that matter of their fathers). Their radical declarations of independence flowed on the swift currents of their indomitable spirits.

They had their lower social status to thank for granting them this freedom. They came from the recently urbanized peasantry and the working-class. Before racing, they had worked as seamstresses, factory workers, newspaper typesetters, shopkeepers and clerks. A number of them had even performed on the vaudeville stage. Bourgeois women had an entirely different set of circumstances. Their material advantages notwithstanding, they were still wrestling with remnants of the "Cult of True Womanhood," an ideology which dictated that a lady must be pious, pure, obedient, and domestic. Working-class women had always lived on the fringes of such rules: it is impossible to be domestic, for example, when you need to wander the city in support of another lady's household; it is impossible to be pure when you are widowed and must resort to episodic prostitution to put food on the table. Racing women escaped the material constraints that hardened their mothers' lives; they also acted outside the rules and limitations of the wealthy ladies they worked for. They could exist in the world largely unchaperoned, and they could express anger, aggression, and competitiveness more freely. All they had to do was claw their way out of poverty and onto a bicycle saddle. Once they had accomplished that feat, they suddenly found themselves in an exceptional and entirely new social position.

What Does a Bicycle Mean?

Women racers derived a radically different meaning from the bicycle than their bourgeois counterparts. Even if they later became wealthy as racers, acquiring their first set of wheels would have taken a lot of initiative and sacrifice. A bicycle would have cost them almost a year's salary; it was impossible for them to view such a dear acquisition as a mere fashion accessory. To them, it was an object of great longing and meaning.

To consider the relationship between longing and meaning requires alloying the imagination with the solid ore of experience. What this new metal lacks in purity it more than compensates for in tensile strength. I run my characters through this crucible in order to show how racing compels them to renegotiate their expectations around three longings—the longing for glory, the longing for autonomy, and the longing for physical power.

Glory: In the world of the velodrome, glory was measured by the adulation of the crowd and the number of lines you took up in the newspaper. Some sought this attention through winning, while others resorted to histrionics, costumes, and other distractions. Cultural historian Warren Susman helps us understand the various paths to glory when he distinguishes between "character" and "personality": a woman who raced under the banner of "character" followed the model of previous generations, winning glory with the steely edge of hard work, diligence, and resolve; a woman who raced under the star of "personality" embraced the new, winning glory with charm, magnetism, allure, and persuasion. Racers tried to win as much glory as possible; some forms of glory offer richer treasures than others.

Another factor in the quest for glory was the audience's attitude towards the racers. After all, glory cannot just be taken, but must also be given. Since men made up the majority of spectators at these events, much of the initial reaction to women's racing was tainted by misogyny, chauvinism, and misunderstanding. The pursuit of glory did not always go as planned. Sometimes racers had to accept it in forms they disliked; sometimes they were outright denied it.

Autonomy: I have already discussed the incredible freedom the female racers enjoyed. The main brake on their liberty was the machinations of the men who organized their events. The League of American Wheelmen

(LAW), which provided oversight for all bicycle races in the United States, would not acknowledge female athletes. This required women to participate in unofficial events organized on a rough-and-ready basis. There were no standard rules, not to mention track dimensions. Such disorder characterized the running of meets in other countries too, with conditions in France being somewhat better. Women's races, therefore, bore a stronger resemblance to traveling fairs and circuses than to professional sporting events. This cast the shadow of exploitation over every competition. Add to this the youth and inexperience of the women, and the potential for abusing power was very real. There can be no doubt that most of the organizers regarded the athletes as pawns for their personal agendas: the "girls" were valuable only insofar as they could draw crowds, increase ticket sales and generate giant betting pools.

Despite such unpromising circumstances, the racers never saw themselves as victims. Yes, each race was an unequal partnership with an unsympathetic associate, but the women never allowed themselves to be truly wrapped around anyone's finger. They made good money. And there were intrinsic rewards as well—offerings of self-enhancement, self-knowledge, and the construction of individual meaning and identity. These not only surpassed the extrinsic rewards of racing, but they also dulled the edge of the organizers' designs.

Power: The automobile did not yet exist. This meant that racers took the bicycle and pushed it to what they considered the very limits of human power, endurance and speed. They were competitors. How could it have been otherwise?

But the need for speed had noticeable consequences: it produced sweat, frowns, red faces, angry yelling, grunts, flying elbows, and crashes. None of these things were permitted to women, not in polite society. And forget about Victorian attire: you cannot sprint in a dress and crinoline while wearing a corset underneath. No, opening the door to power required women to ignore all the societal prohibitions against revealing their aggression and their bodies in public. True, they were not "ladies," and thus enjoyed different social expectations, but rarely before had female power and speed been exhibited on such bold display. The bourgeoisie considered it excessive, selfish and antisocial. They called it "scorching."

Racing women ignored these efforts to tame them, and they established a world all their own.

So, it was not society or gender ideology that curtailed these women's access to power; rather, it was their own physical and psychological limitations. Competition made these deficits painfully clear: no matter how strong or fast they were, there was always someone else who was stronger and faster. The track became a Petri dish where the cultures of self-centeredness, self-aggrandizement, vanity and jealousy grew. For many, it led to a radical and egotistical individualism, which found its echo in the then emergent ideology of social Darwinism. As competitors who sought to win, they necessarily contemplated how to defeat opponents and surpass personal limitations. They asked questions about how equipment, training, rest and diet could help them win. They also devised strategies for cheating. In such a baldly competitive environment there was little social cohesion. Racers experienced their world primarily in terms of fragmentation, not sisterhood.

But surely some of these women stepped outside the velodrome to slow down and take the bird's eye view. Ceaseless conflict became tiresome. Surely there were better aims. In other words, after a certain point, some women must have realized they were aspiring after more than the finish line. They started appreciating how their feelings, desires and self-conceptions were aligning with the demands of a higher order. Their activity implied something greater than the sum of its parts, and, somehow, the fragments were unified into a coherent and magnificent whole. Exploitation lurked around every corner, accusations of transgression could be heard all around, and they nevertheless felt the gravitational pull of transcendence.

Conclusion

My heroines were wild enough to steer their bicycles straight into the bosoms of giants; some were sufficiently level-headed to admit when they had ridden into windmills instead. The bicycle may have changed the rules and suggested fantasies of superhuman power, but some racers learned to temper their aspirations with the cold facts of reality. Rather than riding into the back alleys of frustration, my heroines learned the true limits of their abilities. Yes, they had to trim their illusions away, but, in doing so, they discovered what true adventures awaited them.

CHAPTER ONE

The Royal Aquarium

London, 18-23 November 1895

I

The Royal Aquarium used to have fish. Yes, there were whitebait, star-fish and conger-eels; there were crustaceans of all sorts, clams and oysters; they had bullheads, pogges, pipe-fish and blennies; in one tank swam turtles and tortoises, and, in another, soaked alligators brought all the way from the Mississippi. For a few days, there was even a live beluga whale brought all the way from Maine.

The great liberals intended to use these specimens to raise the common consciousness. They would edify the drab, the poor and the stupid with the embroidery of ichthyology and herpetology, flecked with threads of marine mammalogy. But they failed. The people didn't care about claws, scales or slime. Interest in the aquaria quickly waned, money ran dry, and, one-by-one, all the animals died.

And so, the Royal Aquarium stood vacant. The tanks were drained, and a crusty, white patina dried onto the glass with frothy, green algae blooms clinging to the corners. A silent, murky gloom reigned.

Before you knew it, gentlemen started luring girls into the shadows for unmentionable transactions. It became necessary to deal with this scandalous situation when the city threatened to revoke the license. Since then, every effort has been made to exterminate the darkness with the hissing flicker of gaslights and, more recently, the humming shimmer of electricity. Now there is no chance of a shadow anywhere in the entire building, and, if you could find one, the management would deny it.

With all this light and all this space, the organizers needed something to show and to tell. Where education had failed, attractions might succeed; so, science was replaced by song, magic and spectacle. For the ladies and gentlemen who originally raised the funds, it was a terrible defeat. It was like tearing down the Crystal Palace to make a new Cremorne Gardens with all its hubbub and hullaballoo. From now on, whenever the Royal Aquarium came up in conversation, it was accompanied by hushes and blushes.

So now the great, vaulted Royal Aquarium is filled with sound. It comes from several sources and directions. The "Human Horse" kicks out a tune on the harmonium. Señor Lopez twangs away senselessly on his mandolin as Señorita de Siro adds to the mayhem with her songs and dances. The Dancing Elephants stomp a wistful ballet, the King amidst the Living Fire declaims an impassioned abdication, and Argo the Phrenologist establishes hierarchies through the appraisal of skulls.

And then there is the sham music hall off to the side where maudlin songs spill out to lure crowds to coppery bitter. The round tables stand at just the right height for fist pounding. But the chocolate paint picked out with navy stripes is too staid. No one can love this place! Where are the golden tassels, crimson curtains, shimmering looking glasses and marble pillars? Where is the chandelier? Where are the plate glass doors to walk through so you can feel special when you enter? The songs need some building up, something regal and excessive to go along with your tender feeling. With this arching iron ceiling laced with glass, you might as well be drinking inside the belly of a whale.

It is so loud you have to wonder why anyone bothers. Physical humour and slapstick work best—serio-comics, performing dogs, eccentric juggling knockabouts and lightning artists. W.C. Fields and Harrison can barely get a chuckle. "Don't laugh!" they warn. "Our jokes are dangerous! Unlawful!" The audience complies, but not because they fear arrest. Hercat the Conjurer does his best to work in mime, wise choice, but eventually he needs the audience's ear: he has that story about his mentor, a mysterious itinerant sorcerer with the exotic headpiece and dreggy beard. No one can hear, but they can guess what he's saying. And, really, who thought Grieve the Ventriloquist would be a good idea?

The greatest noise of all is the audience. It gasps at the Human Arrow—a beautiful girl shot from a bow. It stutters during the Great Dives and laughs at the Legmaniacs. It mocks the Harrison Palmers and cheers the Marvelous Boxing Kangaroo. It slaps a knee and guffaws when William Downes comes out of the egg.

And yet, somehow, despite all this entertainment, a grumbling sense of dissatisfaction pervades everything. It feels as if there is a spirit here—a weird one, with giant and hungry ears. It can never hear enough. It can never have enough sound. It always pleads for more, for louder. How cruelly this *genius loci* must have chortled when all the animals died, how eagerly it must have watched as their silently flapping gills halted, and how impatiently it must have marked time as its dream of ever-expanding pandemonium slowly replaced the silence and the darkness of by-gone times. Now it sits and waits for someone to come along and finally fill its cauldron past the brim. All it will take is just one more sound, but it must be the right kind…

Perhaps the lady racers can satisfy this demanding deity. They just arrived with their bicycles, their muscles and their dreams. They pierce the racket with the bumping hum of rolling rubber on loose slats of wood, the crackling of falling bicycles and the bright, sharp glitter of female exclamations made in sailor-mouth French. There is even a band accompanying them. It brandishes its brass with locomotive vigour, and it beckons all to come and witness.

This Ladies' Race is the crest of a wave that has been building all summer long—races at Hull, then Scarborough, then Greenock, then Edinburgh, then Plumstead; now the Royal Aquarium in Westminster. The attraction—women riding in circles like marbles spinning round a soup-bowl, only this bowl has a rim six feet high fenced in with railings to stop them from flying off.

Black fountains preside at each of the track's two bends. They will froth and bubble as the women race by, so that these two tall sentinels will stoically witness every single hairpin turn. And there will be a lot of them (Monica Harwood, the winner, will pass each fountain 3712 times). At their base, stands a panoply of placards. They advertise bicycle brands and the entire carrier wave of cycling accessories and products. Little cherubim reach out between the signs to endorse these trinkets with their mirthful rococo curlicues and pudgy fingers. The competitors will pass so close they might reach out to these little angels and tickle their tummies.

Twelve women have travelled all the way from France and Belgium to race eight English women. The race organizers had actually sent recruiters to Paris, such was their reputation. The French race all the time. One of them is particularly famous—Mlle. Lisette. The others fear her because she recently finished eighth in a sixty-two-mile race in the Bois de Boulogne. She was the only woman, and she trailed the winner by only seven minutes. Mlle. Victorine Reillo is another big name. She comes with the reputation for great speed. She has already beaten Mlle. Lisette twice, and she comes to London to do it again. With contenders such as these, the Royal Aquarium can stoke the audience to new heights: if before it settled for melting wax, now it can try to melt iron.

The continentals have more experience, and their inherent sense of *liberté* make them completely different from the English. They are lively, quick to take offense and are "appallingly garrulous." On the track, they lord their numeric superiority over *les filles anglaises* and yell back and forth like they own the place. It is bizarre to hear hoarse and husky female voices conquer Westminster with French. Few understand exactly what the women are saying, though everyone gets the point.

"*Pourquoi est-elle toute attachée dans ce corsage!? Comme un prisonnier.*"*

"*Et regardes ses rubans! Quelle fillette mignonne!*"†

They blow kisses at the attendants when they receive refreshments, but then they hammer them with unfettered *sacrées dames*‡ when their wants

---

* "Why is she all tied up in that bodice!? Like a prisoner."

† "And look at her ribbons! What a sweet little girl!"

‡ "Sacred ladies," normally in the singular, referring to the Virgin Mary.

are not met. The Belgian Hélène Dutrieux smokes in public. She looks sixteen. Fanouche Vautro crashes on the first day. She, pale and panting, implores her trainer to drop the sponge and get her some cognac. He complies, and she hastily inhales a tumbler before she gets back on the track. She trails Reillo's wheel for a few laps, but finally retires for the day.

The French deliberately make their opponents fall, and then they sprint off without a care while their victims pick themselves up from the boards. Already on the first day, Lisette and Reillo cause Mrs. Grace to nosedive into the planks. The men in the crowd can't believe their eyes. They get angry and start yelling. Those two French jockeys ignore their taunts, but Gabrielle Étéogella won't be restrained. She stops to give the men a few lessons in French which stun them into silence. But she is a hypocrite. She is willing to break glass whenever the English copy her tactics. From behind Monica Harwood, you can always count on her exasperated screech: "*La corde! Nom de Dieu, la corde!*"*

The English are so polite. When the French block them, the best they can do is say, "Now you Frenchies keep to the side and give our girls a chance." They are more reserved because they are less experienced. Many, like Monica Harwood and Rosina Lane, are racing for their very first time. Eleanor Hutton is only fourteen years old. At first, they are confused by the French tactics. But they learn quickly; soon, they yell back at the Gallic amazons just as heartily and heartlessly.

The strategy of deliberately making others crash finally earns penalties for some of the riders. Reillo and Solange are temporarily disqualified for making Rosa Blackburn crash. It is the second time in an hour, and the judge finally decides to take a stand. Solange stoically accepts the judgment, but Reillo becomes indignant and weeps bitterly. She points angrily at the referee and yells melodramatically, "*Il a tort, le diable! Je n'ai rien fait de tel.*"† Reillo loses nineteen miles and all hope through her temporary disqualification. The audience finds her penalty entirely deserved and her behaviour very entertaining.

---

* "The inside. In the name of God, give me the inside!"

† "He's wrong, the devil! I did nothing of the sort."

2. Hélène Dutrieux

The race is popular. Attendance is consistently "immense" all week long. Obviously, there is something to see here.

Up in the balconies gleam the whitest collars and drape the darkest tweeds. Scented mustaches crown fine rows of white teeth as handsome faces cast imperious glances down on the women. Dignified and untouchable, they offer reserved smiles. They only move to straighten out their clothing or to blow their noses into their monographed silk handkerchiefs. They each paid a "lordly guinea" to get up there. This crowd reaches very high, indeed: Prince Francis of Teck and other members of royalty have been seen on more than one occasion.

But these high rollers are in the minority. Most of the men are common. They pay "the humble shilling" to get in. At first, they sit behind their superiors, but they soon start wandering wherever they want. These men have dull, shabby collars, crooked teeth and loud voices. They holler when they think the French are cheating: they throw gestures and get all red in the face. They roar when their English "girls" are winning.

On the final Saturday, prices climb even higher; nevertheless, the place is packed. Enthusiasm reaches such a pitch that some of the nobles start losing their earlier composure: a "well-known sporting Duke" takes a whole row of stalls "at a fabulous price." He's taking his entourage out on a spree, dispensing with dignity for the day. But no one notices. The rest of the audience is so focused on the race that the metal mickeys, inappropriate quips and hearty snickers might as well have been dust.

No one notices the nobles because the women's race has excited the male spectators. They jump back and forth from vexation to joy and from intense focus to dizziness. They are grooms in front of a great white veil. Behind is a face they already know, which, once the veil is lifted, they will see again as if for the very first time. But they're not quite ready to appreciate this. What could knock them out of their slumber and into the cold waters of awareness?

For now, they will settle in and watch the women's violent falls and crashes, which one paper characterizes as "the spice of peril in a performance." To be fair, there are not yet any proper words to describe these falls. There are "upsets," there are "spills" and there are "nasty croppers."

Sometimes riders get "unhorsed" and one woman comes to "signal grief." There is no proper vocabulary because no one has ever seen women fall so violently before. Prior to this, ladies' falls had always been social, and no one believes they can describe these falls using that old lexicon, well-established as it may be.

The tumbles are so numerous and shocking that the press starts to wonder if anyone will actually finish the race. Questions about the sanity of the racers and the correctness of the entire meeting arise. In the *Manchester Evening News*, they say,

> The contest between lady cyclists at the Aquarium seems to be regarded rather as an amusement than a genuine race. The riders themselves are serious enough, but the constant bickering that goes on, and the little tricks resorted to by the French competitors to gain an advantage over their English rivals, are providing the spectators with continuous amusement and the management with no end of worry.

In the *Western Morning News* there is scolding:

> Whether their object is to gain notoriety or money, it is an equally foolish experiment.

And in the *Leeds Mercury* there is both worry and derision:

> The spectator is divided between a profound concern for the women's personal safety, repeatedly endangered, and an irresistible propensity to laugh at their unparalleled eccentricity.

Surely this is not a race, but a ridiculous freakshow, because what is on display is neither competition nor athleticism.

No, it is an attack on womanhood itself. Excessive physical exertion and exposure to constant danger—neither is the correct station of women.

There is the moral element to consider as well: a woman's purity and dignity are more easily exhausted than her muscles and heart. Just read for yourself:

It is doubtful whether women are consulting their own dignity, or increasing popular respect for themselves, by engaging in this rough-and-tumble sport. A public exhibition of female "scorching" is not attractive. Woman is not built for competition in feats of strength... As a race meet, the Aquarium business is a farce.

"Cycling Gossip," Weekly Dispatch.

If the prohibitive taint of hopeless vulgarity is at once associated with bicycle racing for women, so much the better for the physical welfare of those who might otherwise have been tempted to turn a pleasure into a branch of athletics.

Retford and Worksop and North Notts Advertiser

A good many people, no doubt, mindful only of the race athletically, hope the English fair will win; but we know also that a good many people, mindful of the welfare of the race physiologically, will be just as well pleased to see our English women discouraged from attempting feats on the cycle that unduly wear and tear the human frame.

Peterborough and Hunts Standard

There ought to be a society for the prevention of cruelty to female riders

The People

These Amazons of the wheel have vindicated their right to be respectfully considered from the point of view of bodily prowess. Whether they have, at the same time, maintained the dignity of their sex is another matter... It is disagreeably evident that public racing by women is not a feature of a liberal education.

Cambria Daily Leader

The women constitute a show that attracts. That it does attract is not flattering to other attractions or to the public.

Pall Mall Gazette

These Victorian men relish a belief they won't ever relinquish—physical equilibrium is the very essence of womanhood. But these women are competing, and their contorted and strained faces reveal their commitment to vertigo, speed and imbalance. They don't care about propriety. They're out to defeat each other, and, in so doing, they're searching for the limits of gravity, of friction, of tension and of momentum. These tests widen and wild their eyes and make their mouths stiff and grim. They call it a "bicycle face." With such a countenance, a person can scrape the boundary of the permissible and get the attention of the gods. With such a countenance, a person can win a race.

What the men fail to understand is that this is not a performance, not some ghastly number at the *Grand Guignol*. The competitors are willing to break bones—their own and the bones of others' too. Each lap is an offering to the collection tray of some higher calling, to some giant tabernacle where all humanity bears witness to the same nameless but eternal mystery. The men fail to see it, but the women are messengers from some mighty realm of eternal heroes, bearers of some spark in the darkness emanating from an ancient and enduring fire.

Perhaps the men fail to feel the glow from those flames because the women's choice of dress distracts them. The Victorian lady aims to be invisible. She wears grey or black. Her head is covered, always. In the Royal Aquarium the racers wear "go-as-you-please" and confront the men with chaos. The French wear tight-fitting jerseys which connect to their breeches, making them look like beefy ballerinas, but without the tutu. Many of them wear coloured sashes around broad, unrestrained waists. Banners of red or white trail behind them like little birds chasing. The English women dress

3. Nellie Hutton

more conservatively than the French, which says little. They wear blouses with porkchop sleeves decked out with pretty little ribbons tied around their elbows with tiny bows like blossoms. Miss Nellie Hutton wears tight satin breeches, embroidered stockings and an elaborate blouse with a scarf.

Monica Harwood ties the Union Jack around her waist. Not to be outdone, Lisette gets her silk *tricolore* shoulder sash which *Vélocipède illustré* presented to her for her performance at the Bois de Boulogne. The English women wear their hair "daintily dressed," some with it down, some neatly plaited. The French wear their hair in plain "bobs." Everywhere there is windswept hair and dazzling colour, yes, "all the colours in the rainbow," including "electric blue," a truly shocking colour for 1895.

More shocking than the crashes and the colour and the hair are the legs. The press claims that the competitors "have donned male habiliments," but this statement is made in bad faith. There is nothing masculine to see here. These are women's legs. Some of the French riders do not even "take the trouble to have the upper parts of their breeches baggy." The papers complain about Rosina Lane's outfit, a bifold dress with a queer bodice that makes her chest seem barren and her legs look like two caterpillars. They say that women dressed in this fashion are not good to look upon—and yet they can't stop looking:

> There are some very taking costumes worn, but it is not to be forgotten that some dresses that look very pretty and are well adapted to competition in a covered building, would seem rather *outré* in the open air for practical out-of-door work.
>
> *North Star*

> There can be no exception taken to the costumes, if the event is regarded as an exhibition.
>
> *Coventry Herald and Free Press*

To dress this way off the track would be rebellion.

So, the men in the audience come here to escape the ordinary and to see something not quite permitted. They have come to see the women's muscles and to witness their femurs pumping like locomotive pistons in conjunction with their earnestly bobbing heads and shoulders. They find that they enjoy the witty burns and taunts the women shoot at each other, and they revel in their recklessness, aggression and skillfully calculated risks. All the men shudder at the incessant falls and crashes—one man actually loses sleep! They don't know whether to cheer or to feel indignant when they see the women's angry, passionate faces and hear them groan and pant like dogs. They are astounded by the women's perspiration, and then they quietly pretend not to notice when it spreads to unmentionable places. They take offense at clothing designed for passionate bursts of power and panache, and then they stare at the exact same clothing with improper curiosity and longing. They wonder at the entire scene as if it were the world depicted on Achilles's shield. It enthrals them and they continue admiring it for six straight days. Outwardly, they may call it "vulgar competition," yet, inwardly, they are moved.

And it's clear that they *are* moved because they ask questions; not all of them are stupid.

"Do you know," asked one man, "how much these women get per mile for the work they do?"

"No," said the journalist.

"Wouldn't you like to know?"

"No," said the journalist.

"Then don't you think the reading public would like to know?"

"No," was the response.

"Then I think you're mistaken. Why? Because if the public wasn't interested in the racing it wouldn't take the trouble to come here in such numbers as to pack the building at prices that ought to make ordinary showmen weep. Now, wouldn't you like to know how much per mile the women get for making a record day and a record week for the Aquarium? Of course they are racing for money and other prizes. But you know what that means? Or you ought to know. They announce that a ton of money depends upon the result. Meanwhile, money prizes amount to five shillings or five pounds. Only the winner will take home the hundred pounds."

"Do you suggest that these women are riding a couple of hundred miles or more per week for amusement?" suggested the journalist, a *Pall Mall* representative.

"No," said the other, "I don't, but at the same time I fail to see how they can make one-and-a-half pence per mile pay for wear and tear of clothes, to say nothing of bones, or rather of skin, for no bones have been broken, though why I can hardly imagine, for if men attempted to turn those corners at the same pace there would probably be a few less bicyclists alive today. Of course I'm sure about the one-and-a-half pence per mile. At the start there were twelve Frenchwomen and eight English. You can call them girls if you like, but some of them are no chickens. In the first week a number of them covered about 350 miles. The foreigners came here under contract. According to this, their passage was to be paid both ways, and they were to get three pounds per week. Out of this they were to pay for their board and lodging. Of course they were to find their own clothes. Their keep must have cost at least one pound per week, which would leave them two pounds. If you will divide two pounds by 350 miles, you will find the result about one-and-a-half pence per mile. Only the winners and placed riders could expect to get prizes. How much money these represented I don't know, but not much, it's safe to say. All this makes it seem as if the Aquarium has a very good thing, and the bicyclists something not quite so good. It hardly seems fair, inconsequential as professional female bicyclists may be, that the Aquarium should reap a golden harvest and leave the sowers nothing but the tares."

In addition to reasonable and practical questions, some of the men notice things they had not expected to see. For example, there is a thirty-five-year-old in the race. She is significantly older than the other racers. She has four children. The youngest is almost two. She runs a small watch repair shop in Chelsea with her husband, Arthur George Duerre. This is her first race and she will place sixth. Her legal name, as the press likes to point out, is Mrs. Duerre. Her racing name is Miss Rosina Lane.

4. Rosina Lane

The appearance of the wife of a Chelsea tradesman in a race of this character has naturally excited some talk. A lady who races at all requires a deal of nerve: but when the danger of collisions with French girls, with high gear and low tricks, is added, a lady has to be positively bold.

Westminster and Chelsea News

They only call her a "lady" because she is older. She has absolutely no social standing whatsoever. She was born in 1860 in Gloucestershire. Her father was a farm bailiff and her mother had nine children. When Rosina was twenty-one, she moved from Warwickshire to Chelsea where she worked as a machinist for two years, at which point she married her husband and helped him with his shop.

No one knows why Rosina got into racing. Perhaps it was her husband who encouraged her. He was an enthusiastic cyclist. Perhaps she did it to show him up, as there seems to have been as much rivalry as love in their marriage. She continued racing after this event at the Royal Aquarium. Other notable races took place at the Olympia in West Kensington and at Bingley Hall in Birmingham. Her last race was on 15 August 1898 when she organized an open international race at Putney Velodrome to demonstrate the merits of rational dress and hold exhibition events. Six days after the Putney event, she had a crash with a horse and carriage in Richmond Park, Chelsea. Her body and bicycle became pinned between the carriage and the bridge wall, which then broke and gave way. She and her bicycle fell into the river below. She survived her injuries, but never raced again.

The Westminster Six-Day Ladies' Race ended on 23 November in the afternoon. The total accumulated race time was twenty-two-and-a-half hours. Monica Harwood won the race with 371 miles and two laps. She was nineteen years old. Lisette, the much-feared French master, came in second with 368 miles and six laps. Reillo never recovered from her penalty and finished eleventh with 322 miles and four laps.

In order to find assessments of the race, one must turn to the gossip columns. Harwood's prize was a purse of gold, a gold watch set with diamonds and a diamond half-loop bracelet. Rosina Lane took a purse of gold and a double-crescent brooch. One paper questioned the quality of such prizes: "There was a rare lot of diamonds on show at the prize-giving and hence the suggestion that they were only paste."

Though the Royal Aquarium did initially set the women's payment very low, it seems they only did so because they had no idea how the race would be received. By the second day it was clear that the race was going to be the latest thing, and the organizers altered their agreements with the competitors accordingly. They covered the women's hotel bills and allowed them to eat and drink for free at the Royal Aquarium restaurant. And the organizers were generous: "Tea and toast have not figured largely upon the bills, but soup, roast beef, chicken and bottles of claret have." Harwood actually gained four pounds.

Many of the women did very well after the race. Some got sponsorship deals. Harwood, the winner, got to keep her Atlas bicycle, and Lane got a deal with the Swift Cyclery Co. out of Coventry. Lisette got a deal with the Simpson Chain Company. Now she rides with a chain that looks like a cantilever bridge. One man was so moved by the women, their spirit and their sacrifice, that he actually created new prizes for them out of his own pocket: "I discern a great, blazing furnace operating in these girls. As such, I wish to distribute a little of my wealth among some of them." He didn't seem to know their names very well, so, with the coaches' assistance, he filled out four cheques, each for ten pounds. He gave these to the women with the four highest scores. As he handed out the cheques, someone said, "And Miss Hutton has also ridden very well." The man agreed: "Something must be done for her." He wrote her a cheque for fifty pounds.

II

After the race was over, Victorine Reillo wanted to throw her bike against the wall. Damn those English! Harwood's victory was just beginner's luck. And then that kind man wrote all those cheques, but overlooked Reillo because she was French. She had been a contender, starting the second day in third place. Damn that penalty!

But Victorine never recouped her lost laps. It was impossible. For her, the entire race had flattened into nothing more than an exhibition. An absolute waste of time. Quitting was a very desirable and constant thought, but then there was the matter of that contract. It would have been too expensive to quit.

Damn that horrible and flimsy track! It was so narrow. It was impossible not to send those English chickens off their wheels. No, *les rosbif** should have asked us how to build a track. Then we could have had a proper race!

She tidied herself up, got dressed and invited Gabrielle to join her for a walk around the city.

The two young women walked quietly past the Houses of Parliament and the so-called Big Ben. The sun was shining, but the wind was bitter. Gabrielle was obviously underdressed, and she pressed up against Victorine to keep warm. They would not be walking very far, but Gabrielle insisted. Victorine suggested they walk across the Westminster Bridge to see the Thames.

"We've been here all week, close enough to spit in it, but we haven't even seen it once. Let's go."

"Fine," muttered Étéogella, her voice shivering. "But only halfway. Just to the middle of the bridge. I won't go a step farther than that, Vi-Vi. I won't do it!"

The two young women reached the midpoint of the bridge and looked into the river. The wind grew stronger, but the setting sun was glorious and made everything look golden and supreme.

A slight, middle-aged man, finely dressed with a closely cropped beard, was standing nearby. He was also taking in a view of the river on this winter evening while a carriage waited for him. He said something to the young women with a reserved, but genuine smile.

"No English," said Étéogella, making a brusque brushing motion with her hand.

The man smiled even more, took stock of Reillo and Étéogella, then said in perfect French, "So the ladies have come to see the river." He pointed to the sky and the river. "What a fine view!" He spoke with a heavy Polish accent, but otherwise his French was flawless. He walked slowly towards them with his cane.

---

* *lit.* "roast beef," *slang for* "Englishmen"

5. Victorine Reillo in 1895

"You know, when I was a young man, I used to work over there," he pointed behind the Houses of Parliament. "My friend and I would come down to the river to observe how high it had reached, taking stock of the tidal shifts from day to day." He paused to think. "Yes, the sea comes in every day, sometimes as high as ten feet. Just look at those embankments," and he pointed to the tall wall rising out of the river protecting Westminster.

It was true. La Seine has embankments, but it is always possible to walk below them.

"When it floods in Paris," added the man, "it is because of the rain; when it floods in London, it is because of the sea. Even now the tide is coming in." He looked over the railing, silently admiring the current.

"The English are imperialists," he began, "because the sea comes into their capital. Initially, it was their vulnerability; it has long since become their opportunity. It is a treasure for them to have always known that they were connected to the world and the world was connected to them. Too bad so much of this connection has depended on the self-centered metaphor of the horizon and on the myth that all that lies beyond it is mere darkness, just waiting to be filled with light."

He paused here, not because he wanted to give the women a chance to speak, but because he was thinking about what to say next, how to finish his thought. "The sea might flood London from time to time, but London has ridden this river to go out and flood the world."

"Alright, old-timer. We can see you're a very smart fellow, but how about clearing off and leaving us girls alone?" interrupted Gabrielle as she sharply walked away, pulling Victorine with her. "Weirdo!" Gabrielle muttered, hardly under her breath.

The man was not offended or even surprised. He took out a notepad and jotted something down with a pencil. He turned eastward, admired the sky in the opposite direction of the setting sun, wrote something more and then hobbled back to his carriage.

As Gabrielle dragged her away, Victorine halted in her steps, so that her friend grew impatient, tugged harder, and grimaced.

But the man had said something interesting. There was something there, in his words—not about England. No, who cares about England! It was the river, the tide and the bridge. Wouldn't it be great to wait here until the tide went out, as if such a sacrifice would enable some sort of dramatic personal transformation, as if she could somehow harness the force of the ebbing tide in her heart and legs to use in the next race.

But it was getting cold. Gabrielle was being friendly—for now—but that would not last for long. Her tongue could become very sharp. It took very little for her to say something really nasty. Victorine was not in the mood for it. The poor race result was upsetting enough. Who wants to fight needlessly?

The two women walked back to the hotel, arm in arm, one trying to get away from the cold, the other thinking about the river. As they walked past the Royal Aquarium, now closed, its silence seemed unbelievable. All week long this place had always been so loud and energetic. Now it stood quiet, dark and empty.

Victorine whistled.

6. The Royal Aquarium

CHAPTER TWO

The Festival of Fire

Minneapolis, 5-10 September 1898

I

Sitting alone in her hotel suite, Tillie Anderson flipped through a magazine. On the page was a very ugly commercial: "The Father of the Waters pauses at Minneapolis to turn the wheels of the greatest flour mills of the world." The colossal god stood against the cascading waters, but with a gaunt and toothless face hidden between wispy eyebrows, mustache and beard. His skin, saggy and white, drooped over his still vital muscles— each pectoral was the size of a small ship. His long hair hung from his temples and gave him Sampson's ears, while it was brutally obvious that Delilah had taken the hero's sacred crown. His hands, like two brawny nations, wielded a great wheel. But it was not his wheel. It could not be his wheel because the commercial boasted that Minneapolis's grist mills could turn out 35,000 barrels of flour a day. Even at the level of metaphor, this image fell flat. Here was omnipotence in a harness: Pillsbury commanded the god.

Surely somewhere there must be a legend about this Father of the Waters, about how he was captured and tamed and tethered to a wheel at the base of St. Anthony's falls. He is condemned to repeat the same activity for as long as his captors dictate. The Father of the Waters in the perpetual service of grinding Minnesota's flour. Perhaps in some archive there lies the diary of a monk with a contrarian spirit, and, rejecting Father Hennepin's choice to name the falls after the saint who preached to fish, this Jesuit brother wrote down the true story of this deity, the story about him before the arrival of the mills.

Tillie pursed her lips. What was this advertisement trying to say? Really, these magazines were like those scoundrel peddlers—worse even, because here it was, on the table, in the room. It was not an advertisement, but some kind of invasive hallucination, a fraud. 'The Father of the Waters.' 'Pauses.' Whatever turns those mills certainly never pauses, at least these Minneapolitans better hope it doesn't. And, whatever it is, it certainly is not a man. Tillie smirked. There was that skinny bellhop who had tried to help her check in the day before. The boy had suggested carrying her chest and bicycle in two trips. "I think it's all too much, ma'am," he proposed. Tillie frowned, threw her bike over her shoulder and grabbed the chest to climb the stairs alone. In her large dress, she struggled, and she thought of an angry bear climbing a mountain in search of a den. The bellhop silently slid into the cloakroom at the base of the stairs to hide.

She looked again at the advertisement. "The falls turn your wheel, old man." She got up and did a couple of crisp, snappy squats in her dress.

She looked in the mirror. Her red cheeks danced on her deadly, serious face. What is a racer? A person who wins? Is that all? And what is it to win? And who wins? Can one win and still lose? What about that? What about when I don't win? What then? ... Just give up?

Up until recently, a flush of blood was an adequate trick for moving past questions like these. To vanquish a wandering mind, pound out a physical effort of some sort. Lately, however, kicking herself with this spur was becoming less and less effective. The flush of blood was proving weaker than a certain train of thought.

7. The Father of Waters "Pauses" at Minneapolis

It was difficult to say when it had begun, but this slowly coasting freight progressed with a relentless momentum. It had been chasing her all over the Midwest with a tireless insistence and had followed her all the way here to Minneapolis. Revelation would certainly occur at some point, but when or how remained uncertain. It would not be a race victory or a new sponsorship deal. No. This would be entirely new, and yet somehow also… familiar. Whether it would be a calamity or an Eden, Tillie could not say. All she knew was that the hairs on the back of her neck had been bristling ever since December in a shuddering, nervous chill. She felt it all the time, like a permanent but miniscule electric current running through her: there must be something more to wheels than the legs that push and pull them, more than first and last place.

Maybe.

She did a few more squats.

Phil, her husband, walked into the room. It was good to see Tillie warming up. He paused to admire her: there was the vigour, the determination and the strength. She was back on track.

"I think this race will be your hardest," He said. "Dottie is still angry with you about the press in New Orleans, and then of course there is this Lisette. The papers have gone crazy with her. It's obvious that Mr. Haskell and his minions have already picked her as the winner."

Tillie looked at him with her cold, grey eyes and flat mouth. Phil was used to seeing this face before a race. In fact, he loved it, because, normally, he could see the finish line there; lately, however, all he saw there was a question mark.

"Are you concerned about Lisette?" he asked, trying to make a divination.

Tillie paused before responding: "She is an eccentric, no question, but I don't have much to say about that. It's just a distraction, as far as I'm concerned. As for her riding, I've been watching her train. She is a fine rider, but I don't consider her a threat. I can't imagine her or anyone will be able to beat me," she replied flatly. "And as for Mr. Haskell… well, if Lisette has turned his head, then he is a fool and he will lose a lot of money."

"If you're right, he won't be alone," said Phil. "That French woman has turned everyone's head!"

Tillie paused. She thought about William Haskell—jiggly and perfect, like a bowl of red gelatin dessert straight out of the icebox. But this was just a diversion, a sleight of hand to draw attention away from his hawk-like stare. He was a clown with the eyes of a Pharaoh.

"I think Mr. Haskell is a cunning man," Tillie replied. "He likes to play the fool, but there is a lot going on there that we do not get to see. But I'm no mind reader. Whatever he intends, I know that I will win. No, unless something prevents me from finishing, I will win. He knows this. I feel certain he is counting on it."

"He's playing a very dirty game if you're right."

She threw her husband a condescending smirk. "They all play dirty, darling. You should know that by now."

It just did not make any sense for her to be so moody about imminent victory. True, Tillie had always taken herself and everything she did seriously. But she didn't exactly have a choice. When she first arrived in Chicago from Sweden as a teenager, her survival depended on it. She became a skilled seamstress as quickly as she could. She would work away with her sisters and her mother, crammed into their little shabby apartment in Swede Town, stitching and sewing all the long hours of the day.

She got her gravity from her mother, one of those Scandinavian matriarchs of the Midwest. The Vikings, having died off ages ago, could not have held any power over this woman, for she had inherited the fortitude and authority of her forebears. Not a single circumspect Penelope among them, these wives carried the keys, dictating when their marauding husbands could come home and when they should keep out to sea. The mood for heroics was absent at the hearth. Trophies stayed with the ship or were cached away somewhere on the beach. No one at home cared. The preservation of order and preparation for the winter were the only vocations that mattered. Reaching Kingdom Come was not a trophy that could be seized. It could only be attained through cooperation and long toil. That's why the old folk used to say that a pair of sheep and a mended roof are better than wandering. Tillie's mother believed it. She brought this uncompromising work ethic to America; she pushed her daughters to maintain it. There was no time for leisure, no time for doing anything for themselves, no time to imagine anything other than work. Aspiration was an inexcusable luxury. If you dared to have a second of spare time it was only acceptable to devote it towards acquiring more sewing skills. Anything else was self-indulgence. If Tillie's mother had been the ant in Aesop's fable, she would not have even noticed that stupid, rascally grasshopper to begin with, not to mention speak to it and pronounce judgements: she would have been too busy. With her mother at the helm, the family would survive its transition to American life. That was why Tillie always handed over all her money and leftover fabric. Finances were tight, but the family pulled together. They survived with modesty, but also with dignity.

That was what made Tillie so extraordinary. Dignity, discipline and determination, she had, yes, but modesty was out of the question. Whenever she looked in the mirror, modelling her mother and sisters' work, she never cared about the cut of the dress, whether or not it was correct. And she certainly never cared about whether or not it was tasteful. She didn't ever see the dress. She always saw a person, a special person, a person who could matter to other people and not be hidden away stitching and sewing next to some drafty window. Sometimes she saw a person who was directed towards some sort of greater end; other times she saw a rogue or even a rapacious invader. No matter who she saw, she always saw herself.

Yes, and somehow there was a bicycle at the end of this path. It was, at least in part, social contagion. The bicycle was everywhere, in magazines, in the press, even in penny and dime novels. There were bicycles in the street, too. The answer suddenly appeared simple: in order to escape the dull world of the seamstress, free yourself with a bicycle.

But not any bicycle would do. The dainty ladies riding slowly in Lincoln Park were a sorry lot. How could they be satisfied, being corralled to paths like cattle and chaperoned by fathers and beaus like children? Her clients, wealthy as they were, exaggerated their new freedom. It was a sham. No, the young men, the scorchers, the ones who tore up and down the city streets with such speed, independence and entitlement, who coursed through intersections with such panache and dexterity—they knew true cycling. That was the truth about wheels. Nothing but a diamond frame would do, what others incorrectly called "the man's frame." A diamond frame to generate speed and to demonstrate strength. A diamond frame to make it impossible to wear a dress.

In the meantime, sewing needed to get done. Mother got everything, but allowances can grow into surprising savings when one applies discipline and shocking austerity. Still, it wasn't fast enough. More money was needed, and she took on laundry work to help. Every waking hour was spent stitching and washing and amassing money. In this way, the young seamstress clawed her way out of the sewing room and into a bicycle saddle. By spring, she could afford her first bike. It was bulky and weighed almost half as much as she did. It didn't matter. She finally opened the door.

At first, her mother tolerated the riding. Yes, she noticed a dip in the household income, but she expected the bicycle to be a phase. Tillie had worked so hard to earn it, been so good and so industrious. She deserved a reward.

But who could have suspected that Tillie was sneaking out before breakfast to ride by herself? Who could have expected that her daughter would purchase a man's bicycle? Of course, Tillie would ride a lady's bike. How could she have done otherwise? And it was intelligent: her rides would serve as a form of advertising for the family's seamstress work.

Tillie was too proud to be dishonest, but she was also too intelligent to correct her mother's willful blindness. She led a double life for a few weeks, leaving surreptitiously in stockings and knickerbockers, reading about Lizzie Glaw and training to race and to win. Then Tillie competed in her first hundred-mile race. She won it with ease. It started and finished downtown, and her victory made the headlines. She could no longer keep the true extent of her passion a secret. She had to go professional or abandon everything. To her the choice was clear.

That was not a problem, however, because things worked out very well. She got a sponsorship deal with Excelsior Supply Company and traded in her heavy bicycle for one of their superb "Thistles." With these wheels, she joined the racing circuit. It turned out to be great money. Winning one of the six-day races would earn her two hundred dollars. Even if she got sixth place, she'd earn twenty-five dollars: between her work as a seamstress and laundress, the most she ever earned was three dollars a week. It was a nobrainer. Before long, Tillie was giving her mother an allowance.

Phil met Tillie around this time. He was just seventeen when he helped her adjust her chain tension before a race.

"Excuse me, miss, but if you compete with your chain like that, it's likely to fly off."

She resented this teenage boy for interfering, but she allowed it because he spoke so gently and unassumingly. Also, he spoke to her in Swedish.

She quickly realized that Phil was a genuine mechanic, and, from that point forward, a relationship developed between them. Phil was in awe of her strength and her speed, but mostly he was impressed with her work ethic. It felt familiar. He had been raised by his sister who was also an organized and disciplined worker. She, too, was one of those Swedish matriarchs, and, in Tillie, Phil recognized the traits which he found so appealing and assuring. But with them came the astounding additions of a truly unique talent and a lionhearted spirit. Starting as a mechanic, Phil quickly became Tillie's assistant and trainer. By 1897, they were married.

It was a loving relationship, but a professional one too. During races, Phil would shoot Swedish whispers, telling Tillie about the positions and states of her opponents, when to push, when to hold back. She would always wait for that point near the end of the race when Phil would look down at his feet, as if he were embarrassed, sneak a sharp, breezy whistle through his wispy mustache, and draw a crisp and tight circle in the air with his index finger. This was the signal. Once detected, Tillie seethed and raged and turned and pounded all the way to the finish line. She could have torn down a brick wall.

That was before. Now Phil wasn't sure he could count on her to sprint like that. It seemed like she might just ride up to the finish line, advance to the edge without crossing it, turn to him and ask "what is this for?" and "who are these other women?" It just didn't make any sense, and thinking about it was overwhelming. How can a person change so quickly and completely? Once, not so long ago, Tillie had moved through the world with all the self-possession of a wolf; now, she seemed skittish and easily flustered, like a racing horse carrying a distracted jockey. No, something had changed. As her coach, trainer, handler and husband, it was impossible for him not to notice, but its true character and significance remained hidden. Bringing up the subject brought out silence and glares. Phil learned to tread carefully. He didn't know what was changing in his wife. He didn't even know when it had begun.

Maybe it was that time in Cincinnati at the Music Hall. Tillie's six-day race coincided with Reverend Moody's sermon. The race continued all week-long in the horticultural wing; Moody preached in the central auditorium on Wednesday, the third night of the race. Moody hated cycling, especially women's cycling:

> I don't know what we are coming to! Of course I believe in wholesome exercise, but we Americans are so apt to overdo everything that it often results in lasting injury. And where women overdo it, especially, I should think it would lead to troubles particular to women.

What were these troubles? Was Moody really so concerned about the fertility of a handful of racers? No, surely his objections lay elsewhere, not in the body, but in behaviour. To race is to cultivate aggression and a domineering spirit. To race is to renounce kindness. All that to say that to race is to make something that is not a woman, at least not from the perspective of an evangelical leader like Moody.

But there was another matter. To Tillie, Moody was more than just a famous travelling preacher. She had been a member of his congregation when she first arrived in Chicago. She had attended his Bible classes. She had spoken to him. He had answered her questions. His opinion had always meant so much to her. Surely, he remembered her? Surely, he had her in mind when he criticized women's cycling? True, she wasn't that teenage girl anymore, and those Bible classes belonged in another life. It was no longer possible to accept his authority: to not race was unthinkable. And yet she couldn't help thinking that his criticism was aimed directly at her, and she felt a small shred of self-doubt tug upon her sleeve.

The night before that race in Cincinnati Tillie had a dream. Moody interrupts his own sermon, tells his congregation to follow him, and an angry mob storms into the racing hall. He points his finger at her and the crowd boos and hisses. "She has gone too far!" Even the men who came to watch the race forget about their wagers and start booing and hissing too.

And then it is Sweden and she is small. Her mother gasps and scolds her when she catches her tilting a teacup on the edge of a thrice-folded napkin. She has been folding it over and over again to make a high stack, higher and higher with each fold. She tilts her teacup on the napkin to see how steep she can tilt it before it falls over and the milky tea spills.

Then, she sees her sister. They're together on the Midway Plaisance at the World's Columbian Exposition in 1893. Her sister is too meek to play devil-among-tailors. Tillie just keeps on sweeping mercilessly, brutally, destructively. Her sister says, "Tillie, that's not fair." But it's a game. It's fair. How else are you supposed to play? Her sister quits and Tillie wins. So, they leave the game and find the *tableaux vivants*. Tillie sneaks them into the one depicting a harem. Her sister blushes: "Repulsive. I will never forget the Pasha and the anger he put into my heart." Tillie feels completely indifferent to the harem and the Pasha. In fact, she had completely forgotten about it until now.

With this dream looming over her, Tillie now heard all her mother's objections. Despite all the money from her numerous wins, there she was, practically naked in front of all those men. A seamstress just can't go out in public like that. It's a matter of professional pride. And the men gambled. They gambled on her, which meant they saw her as little better than a horse, and that she was leading them into sin. It simply did not do for a good Swedish and Christian girl, new to this land and earnestly hoping to make her people look irreproachable, to get up and make a show of herself in smoke-filled halls with rumbling wheels and bookies yelling over the din of a marching band. Besides, racing was dangerous.

A few weeks after the race in Cincinnati and the dream about Reverend Moody, there was that other matter of the interview with the highly opinionated Fanny Darling of the *St. Louis Post-Dispatch*.

"I suppose distance truly does lend enchantment to the view," said Mrs. Darling as she entered the drawing room of the Hotel Belvedere. She looked at the young women assembled together on the sofas, dressed in their gay-coloured sweaters and knickerbockers and tights. Dottie Farnsworth was even reclining casually back, taking an entire sofa to herself. Clara Drehmel smiled mischievously, brandishing a ghastly shiner. The new electric lighting painted the racing women in even bolder strokes and colours. Fanny Darling was as dazzled as she was dismayed.

"Now, what would your grandmother have said if she could see the way you are sitting and the way you are dressed?" she said, not addressing any of the women in particular.

"What my mother says is more to the point, actually," replied Lillie Williams, taking the bait. "She is—let's not mince words—shocked. My entire family is shocked. But how else is a person supposed to race? Am I going to wear skirts and a corset and hinder myself in competition just so you can feel more comfortable?"

"Well, I'm not so sure that I am made uncomfortable by your dress. But, since you come to the main point so directly, so shall I: why *do* you race? Let's hear it!"

"At first, I went into this business on account of my health," said Lillie without a moment's hesitation. "When I worked in an office in Omaha, they called me Little Lillie. You could have spanned my waist with one hand, and see," she said, pointing to her broad and strong girth, "you couldn't do that now. And I make much better money racing. I make three to four thousand dollars a year, while as a compositor at the *Omaha Bee* I earned only about twenty dollars a week."

"But what kind of life is this for a girl? Surely you must be harming yourself," Mrs. Darling gestured to Drehmel's black eye by way of demonstration.

"Yes, this life is hard on a woman. I train just like a man preparing for a prize-fight. I get up in the morning, punch a heavy bag for ten minutes and then box for another ten minutes. Sometimes I wrestle and jump rope till I get up profuse perspiration, then my maid rubs me down."

"What!?" exclaimed Mrs. Darling, aghast.

"When I train awheel, I go out, no matter the weather, and I ride wherever I want for as long as I want. The sun, the wind, the rain, the heat, the cold. None of it matters. Yes, this life is hard on a woman, and I think it will eventually break us down and make us old before our time, and yet, I cannot imagine doing anything else. I will continue to race awheel for as long as I am able. I do it to make money and because I like it."

Mrs. Darling was flummoxed for a moment, but she concealed her confusion with a nervous giggle. Then her eyes met Drehmel's and her giggle evaporated.

"Will I introduce you to the other girls?" asked Lillie, locking eyes with Dottie Farnsworth who was still lounging, taking the best sofa entirely for herself. "Well, I guess not," she smirked. "We are hardly on speaking terms with each other half the time. There is much jealousy among us. You know how women are. They are jealous if they are not the ones to get the notice and approval. And these girls will ride a great deal harder for the applause than they do for the prize. Anything to show up the other girl at any opportune time."

Dottie interrupted Lillie with a deep midwestern drawl. "I think that a girl has as much right to ride races as she has to go on the stage." She leaned forward a little as she spoke, but without getting out of her comfortable seating arrangement. "It is hard work, though, and we are called upon to show a great deal of pluck. I have fractured my knee cap as a souvenir of my Kansas City race. Why do I ride with such a knee? Because this is like the stage. You are booked. And once you're booked, you're committed and you're going on the track. Once you start in this business, there is no getting out."

"How would a girl's riding compare with a man's of equal weight and height?" asked Mrs. Darling.

"I think it would be a toss-up," answered Dottie matter-of-factly. "A girl seems constituted to endure a strain of this kind as long as a man, and, I am sure, with equal advantages, it would be a tie."

Next, Mrs. Darling turned to Lizzie Glaw who was wearing pink bloomers with cream-coloured stockings and a matching sweater. A little pink beret sat perched on her head. Despite these efforts, Mrs. Darling frowned. Glaw was the most plain and masculine racer of the entire group. "And what about you? What do you make of your clothes and your way of life?"

"I like this business," answered Glaw, in a pragmatic German accent. "It makes me money and money buys comforts. As for my costume," she said, shrugging her shoulders, "True, it is not very big. *Yah*, I suppose I could carry the whole thing inside a cheese box, but, you see," she gestured to Clara Drehmel who was sharing a loveseat with her, "we all wear 'em. It is nothing special. Our uniform."

Mrs. Darling now turned to Tillie, whom she knew to be the strongest and most serious of the women.

"What do you make of all this, Miss Anderson."

Tillie paused before speaking.

"I have been in eighty-four races and won eighty-two of them," Tillie began confidently and imperiously. "On one occasion I lost the race on account of a broken wheel, and the other time was when Miss Glaw beat me by a lap. I went over and gave her a glad hand, however, as I knew she had won fairly. I won the race on Monday night and had bruises all over me, too, before entering. We're all busted up all the time."

And then she hesitated. This Fanny Darling was a piece of vexatious trouble. Clearly, to her, the racers were just a bunch of brutish monsters. She was using them to help her get a headline.

And who was this woman? What made her so special? This Fanny Darling, so dainty, so fragile and yet pitched so steeply in her judgements? How many dresses had Tillie made for ladies like Mrs. Darling? She still did not understand who these people were or what they were about. They were mesmerizing, the way they claimed to know exactly what was right for everybody else as they hid in the protection of privilege and power. Mrs. Darling—whoever she was, one thing was certain—she was a fake. She pretended to be a heroine of piety and domesticity; meanwhile she was a successful journalist, had an independent income and had scores of readers following her. She told a story about women at home, but her own life involved publicity, money and respect. How could her audience not appreciate this? They would all sit at home reading this interview, shaking their heads in judgement and disapproval. Could they not see the hypocrisy?

Tillie turned to look at the black eye on Clara Drehmel's smiling face. Clara looked beaten. It was sad. It was not as if Clara's face would be improved if it were tidy, flawless, pretty and uninjured. No, and yet, this black eye was a problem, as if Tillie had punched Clara. But a punch is deliberate. Clara got her black eye in a fall. Causing a fall is not the same as punching a face. Why feel guilty?

Now, punching Fanny Darling—hard, with absolute forethought and thorough intention, that was another matter. From a certain perspective this seemed permissible and even desirable. Tillie smiled.

Perhaps there would come a time when it would be necessary to give Clara Drehmel another black eye. Maybe Tillie would get the black eye next time. I suppose all the girls should get a black eye at one time or another, like an initiation into a sisterhood. Who knows? It was confusing. Where did all this racing, violence, aggression and venom lead? Is that all there is? There must be more to wheels than finish lines and the pitched struggles it takes to cross them.

Tillie rubbed her chin, and then she asked out loud, "Do we ever pull hair?" Suddenly, she had everybody's attention. "There have been some pretty bad fights among some of the girls, that is true." But here she trailed off a little, still rubbing her chin. Then, she collected herself and said out loud, "I have won so much that I have nothing to be jealous about. I take excellent care of my health, whether I am racing or not, and if all the girls would do as I do, I think that many of them would ride better." Arms akimbo, Tillie confronted the other racers defiantly—discipline and hard-won success, the seemingly unassailable deities of a golden age, rested comfortably on each of her shoulders.

Dottie and Lillie threw Tillie a glare, and Clara Drehmel's face went sour and dark. Lizzie could not recall Tillie ever extending her "glad hand."

A few days later, a doctor, a reporter and an illustrator showed up at the Belvedere Hotel to inspect Tillie Anderson's leg. The doctor had come to offer a physical evaluation, and the journalist and the illustrator were eager to learn the results—for publication. Tillie agreed to do this, but she wasn't sure why—a postscript to the Fanny Darling interview? Probably. Realizing that her leg would appear only a few days after the interview and in the same paper made her smile. Let them talk! Who cares? She, dressed only in knickers, slippers and a housecoat, presented her bare leg to her guests.

"Really, is this necessary?" Phil chewed his mustache. He didn't understand. He wanted to support her. He loved her completely and was entirely committed to her success as a racer. But things had taken a very odd turn.

Looking at her leg, the doctor concluded that it was a very healthy one, if a little too muscular and sinewy for a girl. It ought to be considered masculine, said the doctor, to curtail his embarrassment. But his diagnosis was made in haste. In his excitement, he had forgotten the essential truth about all legs: use them and they will grow stronger.

After the men left, Phil took a deep breath. An odd turn indeed. He flipped through the mail and found a letter on elegant stationery from Minneapolis. It came from a certain William Edwin Haskell. It read:

8 December 1897

Most Esteemed Mr. Schoberg,

It is extremely irregular for me to contact you directly like this, but it is remarkable just how important it is that I reach you. Really, it is impossible to think of anything more important, as you shall soon have to agree.

I received your St. Louis coordinates from the inimitable and equally esteemed Mr. J. Robertson Smiley (everybody knows him). I have invited the Cycling Carnival Company to Minneapolis this September for this great city's Industrial Exposition, which occurs here every September (to offer Minneapolitans an appropriate alternative to the absolute and total catastrophe which constitute the yokels' quaint festivities at the state fair in St. Paul, a basic horse and cabbage show), to participate in a Ladies' Six-Day race extravaganza spectacular. There will be thousands and thousands of unforgettable memories made in this race. Some of them will be yours and some of them will be Miss Anderson's. I am counting on the fact that some of them will be mine too.

It is impossible to imagine this race without the participation of Miss Anderson. You cannot fail to appreciate this, nor can I.

Many, very many, of the very best Minneapolitans have rallied behind this race to gather funds for the prizes. Believe me, the money will be huge.

Of course, the race would be pointless without the participation of Miss Anderson.

Yours, most sincerely,

W.E. Haskell
    President, Manager and Editor-in-Chief
    Minneapolis Times
    Organizing Director
    Minneapolis Industrial Exposition

Phil hesitated for some time before responding to this unusual letter. Eventually, he sent a telegraph:

Date: 6 February 1898

Attn: W.E. HASKELL

HOW MUCH PRIZE MONEY?
WHO ELSE IS COMPETING?

Signed: SJÖBERG

II

On 5 February 1898, the jury reached its verdict. William Edwin Haskell had been in court since mid-December. He, as the Editor-in-Chief of the

Minneapolis Times, had used his paper to publish an affidavit, in which he accused a certain Samuel Hill of grand larceny and conspiracy. But the affidavit completely missed its mark: not only did it fail to cause any action to be brought against Mr. Hill, but it actually required the State of Minnesota to charge Mr. Haskell with criminal libel.

It was impossible to test the truth of either side's claims, but the following seems certain: Samuel Hill, as Director of the Minneapolis Trust Co., had sold a defunct company's bonds for ten cents on the dollar when the creditors begged him to sell them at sixty cents on the dollar. Mr. Hill went ahead against the passionate pleas of the creditors, and, shortly after that sale, Mr. Haskell used his newspaper to publish his affidavit in an attempt to shave off the healthy beard of Mr. Hill's reputation.

No one could say if it was stupidity or simply a brutal lack of concern, but Mr. Haskell did not seem to understand what an affidavit was. You can say you saw cows jumping over the moon to eat honey out of a meat packer's pocket, swear to it in front of any notary public who is more eager to collect a fee than to tell the truth, and there's your affidavit. That in no way compels any court (or any human being) to accept its claims as fact. It was stupid. Mr. Haskell almost invited the state to press charges.

The jury was in deliberation for nearly twenty-four hours before it returned with its verdict. The judge read the decision quietly and slowly, gave the foreman a quizzical look, and then he handed the document back to the clerk.

"We, the jury, find the defendant William E. Haskell, not guilty, but believe that the comments he made in the Samuel Hill Affidavit were excessive."

"What does your verdict mean?" asked an incredulous journalist, not affiliated with Mr. Haskell's paper. "Does it mean, 'Not guilty, but don't do it again'?"

"Oh, I don't know as it matters," said one juror.

"But it doesn't make any sense!"

"Well, I think the jury understands the matter in different ways," offered another juror. "But we decided not to tell how we voted. Anyways, it's over."

Journalists pushed and prodded, and there was some insinuation of foul play, but it all worked out favorably for everyone in the end: Mr. Haskell was found not guilty of libel, and his allegations against Mr. Hill and the Minneapolis Trust Company were ignored. Everyone went back to business as usual and would continue to do so until the muckraking journalism of Lincoln Steffens finally exposed the corruption of Minneapolis city bosses and papermen in *McClure's Magazine* in 1903. Of course, by that time Haskell had gone out west somewhere and even Sam Hill had left too. He cursed his time in Minnesota and vowed to write a book about it, which he imagined entitling *Forty Years in the Wilderness*.

For the reclusive journalist and publicist William Edwin Haskell, the verdict came as no surprise. He descended the courthouse stairs with exactly the same confidence he had paraded for the entire proceedings. There was no doubt that he would win. A paper man, he held considerable clout in Minneapolis. There were his powerful superstitions too: bourbon and sexual abstinence enable a man to control fate. The drink was almost as easy to procure as the train and ocean-liner tickets for his wife to Hawaii. Solitude and bourbon—some will call this mystification. Others will call it doing what is necessary to defeat your foes and to get what you want.

With the libel case behind him, Mr. Haskell could now focus on two seemingly unrelated tasks: one, to jump on William Randolph Hearst's bandwagon and use his paper to push the United States into direct conflict with Spain, and, two, to organize that year's Industrial Exposition taking place in September.

As far as the first task was concerned, there was no shortage of opportunity. Even as early as January, it was clear that US public opinion took offense at the very existence of the Spanish Empire. America was growing weary of its isolationism. It was fed up with licking its wounds from the Civil War. Expansion was now the new word. It really would not take very much to push the country into war, and the hawks and jingoes swooped in to set the stage. All Mr. Haskell had to do was publish the bigger papers' stories in syndication (or just plagiarize them).

Cubans wanted national independence, but the Spanish army quashed their revolts. The American reading public wanted details. One correspondent watched a young Cuban mother die of starvation in a Spanish prison camp, only to be followed shortly after by her infant. This story really stoked the embers of sentiment. Even many moderates joined the cause. The problem was the correspondent completely fabricated the story. He hadn't even set foot on an ocean liner, much less on Cuban soil. There were many stories like these. It didn't matter if they were true or false; all the story had to do was push the "freedom agenda."

Mr. Haskell followed suit: "The United States is on the verge of a crisis, for the temper of the Spanish people is unmistakable, and Spain will not dare concede what we are certain to demand." What followed were a stream of articles about the US army and navy, intelligence gathering, troop readiness and naval positions. The American armed forces were physically superior in every sense. More importantly, the US was morally superior too. The Spanish worldview was tainted. Who better than the Americans to appreciate how insulting it is for a people to be subjugated to the crushing weight of a monarchical and imperialistic power? The United States must intervene so that the bounty of republican virtue can reach these Cuban victims of oppression.

All that was necessary was a confrontation, some great event to open the door into a new era. Frankly, it was biological: the lion with the largest mane always chases away the old grey-headed codger. The press pushed Washington as hard as it could, but President McKinley could not be moved. No war, not on my watch.

Then, a miracle happened: the *Maine* sank in Havana Harbour. And even though "nobody outside a lunatic asylum" actually believed that Spain was responsible, all the newspapers insisted now was the time for the US to intervene.

So, the US finally went to war with Spain, and then it was even easier to sell papers. Everyone wanted to see what happened next. Everyone counted on the telegraph lines to bring in the details quicker than ever before. Everyone looked at the illustrations and even the occasional photograph. Everyone, in the thrall of combat stories, wanted more.

Then, when no one thought it could get any better, another miracle happened—Theodore Roosevelt took San Juan Hill, and ended every public statement with "I'd just like to add that not a one of my men so much as flinched." Roosevelt had actually shot a Spanish soldier dead with a pistol reclaimed from the sunken *Maine*. When someone suggested he shot a retreating soldier in the back, Roosevelt countered with a big smile: "I clipped him in the left breast as he turned." In this way, Roosevelt came back a hero. Even though his active duty lasted less than a summer, and he saw less than two days of combat, he demanded to be awarded a Congressional Medal of Honor. It just kept getting better and better. Really, the articles almost started writing themselves.

By the summer of 1898, the United States had taken its fill of Spanish colonies—Guam, Cuba, the Philippines and Puerto Rico. But it wasn't finished yet. It wanted a little bit more, and so in August it annexed the sovereign Republic of Hawaii. After that, the jingoes all agreed: it was time to stop.

No one of consequence was calling this humbug or hokum. No one thought of it as a dangerous poison. No one even thought of it as imperialism. It wasn't "the bald eagle's talons digging" into the Philippines or Cuba; it was the "setting afloat of miniature American constitutions" in the Pacific and the Caribbean. And anyone who dared suggest that such behaviour was somehow anathema to a republic was just being needlessly muddle-headed. "These anti-war ideas emanated from sources that could not be described as patriotic or loyal to the great American flag," wrote Roosevelt in the papers. Obviously, America had every right to reach out and take whatever it could. Capability was justification. In fact, capability made it a scientific necessity. The stronger must always smash the weaker. To do otherwise would invite the conquerors to our own shores.

As far as Mr. Haskell was concerned, the war with Spain had become connected to his second great task of 1898—organizing the Industrial Exposition in September. Dovetail it into the promotion of America's military successes in 1898. One would promote the other, and, besides, Haskell had already completed most of the organization work anyways. All the main attractions were committed and lined up. Now, instead of the mindless thrall of every other September, they would all be channeled into the celebration. All the attractions to celebrate all that victory. Most important of all, he had the commitment of the women racers with the Carnival Cycling Company. He had even managed to get Tillie Anderson.

Was there something to connect his city's annual celebration to the nation's successes of 1898? He needed to come up with an image. It had to be something dramatic, something lively and celebratory, not to mention true. Very true. There was only one choice, really.

Over the course of the summer, there had been a tendency amongst the young soldiers to desecrate the graves of the people they had liberated. Photographs of American soldiers holding Filipino, Cuban and Puerto Rican skulls as trophies appeared in postcards, albums, newspapers and magazines. There was that dandy one of the young private with three skulls. He squatted playfully holding one in each arm as he balanced the third on his head. There was that other one with the three privates holding skulls in front their dark uniforms: the young men looked like living pirate flags. Yes, that killjoy General Brooke ordered his men to stop the bone collecting. True, the boys did not exactly have the consent of the governed, but they can be forgiven for their zeal. After all, they were celebrating.

No matter. It would still be possible to play with those bones here in Minneapolis. With a paper man anything is possible. And here it has to be skulls. Parading American strength with the talisman of another's mortality is far more satisfying than publishing trumped up affidavits. A flaming skull will be the face of the Industrial Exposition in 1898, the most remarkable of all years.

But we can't call it the Industrial Exposition, not this year. There needs to be another name. America has beaten down Spain in a giant confla-gration spreading from the Pacific all the way to the Caribbean. Luzon burned, San Juan Hill burned, the whole island of Puerto Rico burned. American ambition is a blazing fire, purging a path of righteousness all the way around the world, and it has left a trail of skulls in its ashes. The British quaintly claim that the sun never sets on their empire; the American ideal is Good Everywhere. Our republican virtues and our market forces, all the way around the world. Establish Good Everywhere. Oh, and we had. Triumphantly so.

8. Festival of Fire Admission Button: Good Everywhere

So, it is only natural to rebrand this year's Industrial Exposition as a fire. An Exposition of Fire. No, a festival. This is a celebration. A Festival of Fire. The Festival of Fire. The Fire Festival.

Picture a great human skull with missing teeth encircled by a ring of fire. That is the image. That is the talisman, the mascot. Just imagine! This image pinned upon every lapel and bosom in Minneapolis. Oh, Lord! It would be necessary to spend the evening with some bourbon to divine the depths of its true meaning. Thankfully, his wife was busy entertaining guests from the Nineteenth Century Club. It would be possible to jump right into this skull and this fire.

"'Fire Festival' is the word on every tongue," he composed. "Its spirit is in the air. Everything is subordinate to it. Never before has a western carnival celebration attracted such universal interest and attention. Everybody takes it for granted that this celebration will eclipse all celebrations of the past. The people look forward to it expecting a surprise, and they will certainly be surprised. Surprised beyond anticipation by the magnitude and scope of this Festival of Fire!"

Where does one learn to write like this? His father? No. His father, Edwin, was a different sort of journalist and a self-made man. He learned the paper trade during the Civil War when he started the *Boston Herald*. He had nothing—just youth, drive and a willingness to do what needed to be done in order to succeed. Those first issues were all printed on old and worn moveable typeface. He had rescued the metal letters from some government agency before it had the chance to melt them down. Blown, chipped and withered by years of service, they told barely legible stories. Even the headlines bled a little. But there was no shame because that was what a young man did: he anxiously exuded hard work in order to get ahead. He couldn't possibly have gone to war. He was too busy writing about it.

War, be it civil or otherwise, is a story you can run with; Edwin Haskell ran very far indeed. Before long, the *Boston Herald* could buy proper printing facilities, and, even before the Civil War had ended, he was a wealthy and influential man. He rode out that success in the years after the war, until, one day, he sold his Boston assets. He went west and purchased the

Minneapolis Tribune with his friends in order to give his son his first real job. Straight out of Harvard, and young William was already the Managing Editor of a daily paper.

Edwin got his son his first job, but he did not teach him how to write. That honour went to the cabal of aggressive, rowdy, horrible and hard-drinking writers that had followed Colonel Alden J. Blethen to Minneapolis from Kansas City. They were called Blethen's Cowboys, and they changed journalism in Minneapolis forever. There was Abbott Blunt, who got his stories with fists and altercations in the saloons. Chuck Barlow wasn't happy unless his stories ended with a stiff neck, cold as a wagon wheel caught in a rough slipknot noose. It was John H. Leonard who always followed every child abduction to its horrifying conclusion. Ever categorical, Charles Alf Williams never wavered: St. Paul was a den of stuffy, insufferable, disingenuous and uncooperative cronies. And John J. Flynn catawamptiously chawed up all the Wobblies in all their attempts to establish unions at the flour mills.

Young William had a wealth of experience to draw from, but the rowdy Cowboy who had the strongest influence on him was certainly R.B. He always took "Billy" aside to offer him bourbon and advice.

"You know, I've heard some people say it was a dart and a map on the wall that informed Blethen's decision to bring us to Minneapolis. That's the story, I swear. Sometimes, important decisions can be made in this manner. A fatalistic and mystic symmetry. Yes, symmetry, because with a pivot of the forearm and the flick of the wrist, the flying dart and the map reveal the contact of human will with chance."

"My father says Blethen came here to escape the typography unions in Kansas City," interrupted William.

"That is a dreadfully amusing potentiality," guffawed R.B. "Absquatulated with his Cowboys to Minneapolis to escape the reds, did he? Rode out on the rails, chased by the Wobs? That sure is some pumpkins, boy. Some pumpkins, indeed! But there is not one shred of truth in that spick-and-span proposition."

"Why not?"

"You know, for a boy entering the paper trade, you sure got a lot to learn," R.B. sat up, straightening out his coat and vest and adjusting his tie. "Listen Billy," he continued, "if you want to be a paper man, you got to learn how to bend." He looked at young William Haskell meaningfully. "I mean you got to bend things—bend them with your paper, and bend them so hard they get bent.

"Bending just means that you have wrought a favorable result. There is a litany of 'favorable results' you might aim to fashion with your writing, but the main result that you must always have in your sights is selling. Because no matter what happens in the world, the only thing that matters to you are your sales. You follow my advice, Billy, and you won't regret it.

"The readers?" He took a swig of bourbon without taking his eyes off William. "They're not worth the tears. Besides, what are you doing exactly? You're drawing pennies away from the saloon and into your pocket, and for what? The common good. Because information is always to the good, son. Don't forget that. We're the good guys.

"Back in Kansas City, we had no difficulty selling papers because we always bent everything that came across our desks. Christ almighty, we churned those stories out like daisies on a daisy chain. We got so skilled in our trade that some days we couldn't keep up. Why, there was one time we got so drummed up bending stories that it nearly cost us our lives. I swear it's the truth!" R.B. emptied his glass of bourbon and continued speaking as he poured himself another.

"A ring of confusion had encircled that outlaw Jesse James. We jumped on that curl and poured out story after story: James dug up the grave of a priest, James shot up the sheriff because he had hairy nostrils, James had an offer of marriage rejected by a pretty girl because he smoked tobacco and James went to Russia to visit the bordellos in Moscow. Pure confabulation! All of it! And, d'you know what? That outlaw came to town to wake snakes, the jackal. There hadn't been a gunfight in Kansas City in a generation, and, now, of a sudden, here was the country's most heinous outlaw on our doorstep. We had done it!" R.B. laughed. "And there he was, Jesse James, standing outside our offices with his hand on his holster, waiting. And then he yelled, 'I came here today to settle hash with you, Colonel!' He actually said 'hash.' Can you believe it? No, you can't, because it was unbelievable. I can scarcely believe it myself.

9. William Haskell in his Electric Carriage with his Cronies

"Well, Alden J. Blethen really impressed us all on that day. They call us the Cowboys, but, you know, Blethen is the real buckaroo (even though the old bastard hails from Maine!) He went outside, shook his fist at that filthy scoundrel and told him to scram and never return. And you know what? James walked off. True, he was fit to be tied, but he left. He backed off without so much as firing a round, not to mention uttering a word.

"Now, do you suppose we retired the Jesse James pitches after that? Hell no! He became our running story for weeks. We pushed all we could on him, telling all sorts of details, as coming from our own perspective, of course. And, you know, we ended every story with a reminder that the price of Jesse James's head was ten-thousand dollars. Ten-thousand dollars! We ruffled his feathers with lie after lie after lie, and then we encouraged a generation of hounds to go out and get him! It was brazen madness, but it was our job. We couldn't stop. It was impossible. (Though, between you and me, we were all rather pleased when Bob Ford sent a plug straight up that soap-lock's coot ass! Gone for good he was, and none too soon!)

"But I've fallen a little off the scent now... Bending, it was. We're on the subject of bending. You need specifics, don't you? Well, how do you bend, you ask? The way I see it, there's but a few tributaries that lead to success. First, you are always certain and convinced, no matter what it is you're talking about. There ain't no room for no equivocating in your copy. You are categorical about everything. If you show doubt or any sort of vacillation, you ain't gonna pull it off. Second, opposing facts. They don't count, not when you're writing for your own paper, damn it." R.B. actually paused here for a second. "Well, sure, they exist, but they only count as fodder for the corral. Cast aspersion, no matter what. You always show your opponents' true colours, which is always some variation on the following: they're artful side-trackers, they're determined draggers of feet and champions of difficulty; their ideas are platitudinosities, pure shecoonery and a strong-arm against reality; they are constructors of schemes and heroes of futility; Christ, boy, you straight up say they are wizards with a facility for the black arts. They're the rival, damn it. Make sure your readers see it that way! Third, you gotta know what your readers want, and, if you don't know what they want, (or you don't like what they want), then you make your readers feel stakes. That's the next point. They gotta feel like they're going to lose the roof over their head. Correction, you got to make them feel like they're going to lose everything. And the last point, really just an extension of stakes, is you offer them rewards. I don't mean real rewards—those cost money. I mean offer them the satisfaction of following *the* truth. Offer them the reward of justification. Offer them the reward of certainty. Offer them absolute righteousness. You want to offer them so many of these rewards that their heads go spinning. And how do they know they can count on these rewards? Easy. You're the managing editor. One day you'll be the editor-in-chief. They take one look at you, your certainty, your dress, your success, they read about your wife's expensive doings in the society pages, and they see you going up and down the street in that dashing Thomas Edison electric carriage driven by a chauffeur. Never let them catch you, ever, in a doggery like this one, Billy! In their eyes, you are a paragon, a trump card in the great social heap. And, to them, that means everything.

"Bend then spin. Spin their heads so fast that they can't even feel the floor churning beneath their feet. Follow my advice, son, and they'll be reaching into their pockets and giving their pennies to you. Take the whole boodle, Billy. It's yours. But only if you bend, Billy. I said bend." With that, R.B. dramatically drained his glass and slammed it on the bar.

R.B.'s words had an enormous impact on the recently graduated William, but it was Colonel Blethen, *The Tribune's* Editor-in-Chief, who rounded out his paper knowledge with some advice which remained with him for all of time thereafter.

"Billy, I can see that the paper experience you bring from Harvard has a certain charm, *cachet*, shall I say, but it is clear that you are lacking in certain knowledges connecting the realm of symbolatry to the journalistic trade."

The young William Haskell looked back at the Alden J. Blethen vacantly.

"Billy, you are very effective with words. I can see that you have learned a thing or two from my *protégé*, R.B., but surely you understand that words will not suffice for men in our position. R.B. and my other Cowboys are just story men; we are paper men. We need something more than they do, and, by that, I mean we need a good deal less."

The newly married William still did not grasp Blethen's point.

"You must safeguard all your vital energies," here Colonel Blethen gestured to the room where their wives were seated, "so that you may please the gods. They are watching, as it were, conducting all results to their favorable conclusion. If you ignore the gods, they will ignore you."

William, a man hitherto devoid of spiritual inclination or knowledge, still did not grasp his mentor's point.

"At your time in life, and especially in newly-married life, one might be inclined to devote a substantial part of his vital energies to proximate females, in this case, to his wife. To indulge in certain vitality-draining passions, shall we say. That is very displeasing to our gods, I must tell you. That is why, whenever we are on a promotional campaign, it is essential for you to observe the strictest abstinence." Here the Colonel looked straight and hard into young William's eyes: "Abstinence ensures every victory."

Young William didn't believe it. They were always on some kind of promotional campaign, and if Blethen actually thought his advice would be taken to heart, he was either a fool or just a mindless disciple to some weird quackery.

Whatever the case, when the *Tribune* actually failed to make Minneapolis the permanent location of the Minnesota State Fair, Colonel Blethen was devasted. He called all his senior staff members, one-by-one, into his office to discuss their conduct over the past months, their commitment to the cause and their futures with the paper. When it was finally William's turn, the Colonel was red-faced and shaking. The spring in his office chair creaked in time with the pulsations of his sour mood.

"I know it was you, Billy. Make this right."

"To what do you refer, Colonel?"

"Don't be coy with me, Billy! I know what you did. Tell me you won't be having your firstborn in nine months and I'll call you a liar."

William was silent.

"Make this right, Billy!"

It was then that William came up with the brilliant plan of erecting the Industrial Exposition Building. Its purpose? To surpass and ultimately replace the Minnesota State Fair itself. If Minneapolis couldn't host it, no one could.

This project became the centerpiece of all the journalistic efforts of the *Minneapolis Tribune* in 1885. It was William's idea, but it was completely supported by R.B. and all the Cowboys. It was at the centre of all the Colonel's editorials too. There was plenty of bending and bourbon, and William sent his wife to Massachusetts to spend time with her parents—for as long as was necessary.

And it was not really very difficult to raise the money—one hundred thousand dollars. Backroom deals took care of the details. Then they held a meeting. The outcome already bossed, the night was just an excuse to carouse with a foregone conclusion announced at its opening. Minneapolis would make its Industrial Exposition Building and leave St. Paul in the dust.

> The manifest destiny of the young metropolitan giant of the Northwest is written upon a hundred milestones of its marvelous progress. It is written upon the primal basis of its prosperity—the bountiful gift of nature—its gigantic water power. It is written upon the solid walls of its productive factories, and mills, and workshops; its magnificent mercantile houses; its towering granaries; its numberless hives of thrifty industry; its busy marts of trade; its magnificent educational palaces, and universities, and schools; its glittering spires—the celestial indices of a lofty aspiration and a high intelligence; its broad and glistening avenues; its countless and beautiful homes—the sacred hearthstones around which the virtues of a high civilization fructify and bloom; but above all, it is written on the speaking features of a population inspired by an inflexible faith in the future of their soaring metropolis, and by a liberality—nay, a lavish generosity, which responds to every patriotic appeal or enterprising impulse.

> It was this abiding faith and unfailing generosity which last night inspired a handful of the representatives of our teeming population, at a meeting called at scarcely a moment's notice, to subscribe at a single sitting a sum so

generously proportioned to the final needs of the enterprise, as to warrant the *Tribune* in making the grateful
announcement that the building of an exposition building
in all respects commensurate with the exigencies of the
situation, is triumphantly assured, and that hereafter, as
heretofore, Minneapolis will lead the column of progressive as well as of growing cities; and that the throbbing
pulse of its giant industries will cause the towering edifice
to be erected for their exhibition, to quiver with a newly
awakened and energetic life. One hundred thousand
dollars! This it is which makes our destiny manifest. This
it is which insures our manifest destiny.

Within the year the Industrial Exposition Building was completed,
entirely sprung from William's mind. It stood looming over the banks of
the Mississippi River, its dark, nine-story tower a giant stalk from some
gargantuan and prodigious creeper. The tallest building in Minneapolis
and its latest acquisition—the most recent and most significant transformation in a city of continuous transformations.

All the more reason to be outraged when, shortly after completing
this project, Colonel Blethen kicked William Haskell out of the *Tribune*
for good. It may have been payback for his earlier indiscretions, or it may
have been Blethen's jealous distress that his young apprentice was surpass-
ing him. On the other hand, it may have had something to do with those
unfortunate words about President Cleveland's young wife:

> It is inconceivable that this woman should have married
> the President except to obtain the position of mistress of
> the White House…. It is hard to have respect for a woman
> who would sell herself to such a gross and repulsive man
> as Grover Cleveland, and one with a private record so
> malodorous, for the bauble of a brief social ascendency…

To attack the President was fine—after all, no one denied that his record
stank, and it was no secret that he was twenty-eight years older than his

wife. But to criticize this young woman, such a fine and gentle being, demonstrated a judgment so poor as to be completely unforgiveable. The editorial had been made anonymously, but, as managing editor, William had to take responsibility.

Shortly after William's dismissal from the *Tribune*, his wealthy father removed his entire investment from the paper and poured it into the *Minneapolis Times*. Somewhat later, the *Tribune* headquarters burned to the ground, killing seven papermen. This was remarkable, given that the building had always been considered fireproof. Colonel Blethen was at home when the fire occurred. He took it as a sign and left Minneapolis for good.

R.B. was working late the night of the catastrophe. He often recounted how the flames tickled the ceiling above the elevator doors, slipping through the cracks like a shaggy devil's mane. The staircase had become a chimney. It was a smoky, billowing spiral. To take it was certain doom. The conflagration was just like Nebuchadnezzar's furnace, but R.B. managed to survive by shimmying along a telegraph cable to a pole across the street. Three men tried to copy his manoeuvre, but they were not so lucky. Their combined weight was more than the cable could bear.

III

The contest between the Industrial Exposition of Minneapolis and the State Fair of St. Paul became one of the signs of the onset of autumn. The stalwart defender of agrarian values, the State Fair was a shrine for the gods of self-sacrifice, slow and methodical accumulation, agrarian duties, honest hard work, the sweat of brows, outdoor life, dignity and austerity. The Industrial Exposition worshipped a completely different pantheon: it was the purveyor of the latest enthusiastic demonstrations, the stunning, the fascinating, the attractive, the magnetic and the glowing. It presented the seductive novelty of modernity itself, with offerings from the dominant, forceful, urban and consumeristic mass. More than just fairs and expositions, they were two opposing credos, like antipodes on the face of the Earth itself. But it was obvious that the sun was setting on St. Paul. The State Fair looked backwards even though time moved ahead. Meanwhile,

Minneapolis looked forward—to industry, to progress and to the future. It was obvious who would win this contest because only one side was allied with inevitability: that modernity would be modern seemed needless to say.

For years the Industrial Exposition grumbled against the State Fair, but this year would be different. This year it would be the Fire Festival. William Haskell continued composing his announcement in his mind as his chauffeur drove him in his electric carriage. It was now July, and he had already finalized all the details:

> The program is the result of an amalgamated union of brains, genius and everlasting energy. It is quite beyond the power of mere words to describe the magnitude and the splendour of the events. But the program, with its three monster divisions—The Street Processions, the Exposition Features, and the Exposition Performances— is absolutely prodigious, and, in its completion, it overshadows all previous attempts to furnish a comprehensive and absolutely satisfying entertainment of amusement and instruction.

> Eichmann's magnificent spectacular *War with Spain* will never be forgotten by those fortunate enough to see it. It will be a stupendous pictorial panorama of the great conflict with the Castilian arms which has just closed so gloriously for the American people. In a series of brilliant and beautiful tableaux, staged with all the thoroughness that modern scenic art can guarantee, will be presented all of the thrilling events in that great war. The destruction of Montejo's fleet at Manilla Bay on May the first, the campaign against Santiago, the Fifteenth Minnesota at Camp Ramsey, the march of the Boys in Blue to the battlefield, and a complete picture of "Marching through Cuba" will be the scenes presented. There will be a surfeit of patriotic

songs, and the entertainment will be in every equipment
and in every effect, wholly and emphatically patriotic and
for patriotic purpose.

There will be more, a lot more. There will be the Hawaiian exhibit. There will be relics from Manilla and the Patriotic War and relics from the Santiago Campaign, including "army and navy projectiles used in the war." There will be photos from the Puerto Rico campaign and relics from Cuba, including "the flag floated at the masthead of the *Maine* for three weeks in Havana Harbor."

And there will be even more than that! Visitors will witness the Palace of Illusions with the human spider. They can play devil-among-tailors, or watch the Great Safe Mystery. In the garden they can encounter the Goddess of Roses and actually touch electric light at the Fairy Electric Fountain. There will be a dramatization of Rider Haggard's *She*. In "the Streets of Cairo" there will be wedding marches, whirling dervishes, Kurdish dances, marriage ceremonies, acrobatic performances, fortune tellers, street fakirs, beggars, merchants and donkeys. The De Krekos Bros. will present a Turkish extravaganza with "Oriental aggregation in sword fighting," "mysterious juggleries," and "harem dances and Oriental maneuvers." Next, visitors can get entranced by the Cabaret de Neant, Jahn's latest triumph, with the Café of the Dead, and then they can wander into the Grotto of Hades, only to stumble, finally, upon The White Room of Paradise with "transformations and beautiful harem girls dancing before the Pasha." There will even be an "Old Plantation," a "Spectacular representation of the Good Old Days in the South before the War." It will have "buck and wing dancing specialities," songs and so forth. There will be an "Indian" Village with a tribe of "Winnebagoes" from Black River Falls, under Chief White Buffalo with "bear dances, ghost dances, sun dances, death dances, marriage and burial ceremonies, scalping feasts, resurrection songs, weird incantations after defeat and victory, songs of camp and warpath and every known primitive pastime."

"Not one of these features announced is cheap or tawdry," assured Haskell. "Every detail has been carefully arranged, and the various features cannot fail to impress the audience with the completeness of preparation and the thoroughness of equipment in every detail. A perusal of the program will convince the most skeptical that this Fire Festival is altogether too glorious an affair to miss. Indeed, no person can afford to miss it, for it is the opportunity of a lifetime."

Of all the transformational opportunities at the Festival of Fire, there could be no doubt that the women's six-day bicycle race promised to be the most life-altering: "The great bicycle race, which will hold the attention of the sporting world for six whole days, will no doubt prove to be the attraction *par excellence* of the exposition program. The large amounts of money wagered on the result make it a very important race, and one which will be watched with the keenest interest by the sporting fraternity all over the country." In the largest and boldest letters possible, and with more than enough exclamation marks to make the point, every advertisement hoisted up this race as the centerpiece of the entire week's festivities.

The best *cycliennes* had been mustered from around the country. But that is not the angle that the festival needs. This race needs to be bigger, an international affair. Flags will adorn the waists of these girls, and then the men will gamble even more. After all, their national pride will be at stake. It doesn't matter that half our competitors had no further to get here than you can throw a horse. Ida Peterson and Clara Drehmel grew up here in Minneapolis. No matter. What is a Peterson? What is a Drehmel? They are the Norwegian and the German Champions, of course. We need flags for their waists. Dottie Farnsworth is also a Minneapolis girl, damn it. Nothing to brag about there! But I suppose it's true that we'll need someone to wear the Stars and Stripes. That will surely ruffle the bookies' projections. Farnsworth—The American Champion. Lillie Williams may have come from Omaha, but she won that race in England. She has to wear the Union Jack. Moreover, we'll dub her "the ex-World Champion." Bourbon not yet having entered his calculations, William paused: to display such inspiration without recourse to the magic elixir was truly astonishing. And he hadn't even gotten to the best part yet.

It went without saying that the most important participants in this race were the final two—Tillie Anderson and Lisette.

When William Haskell got Tillie Anderson's commitment to race, he instantly knew she would win. He received the letter from Phil Sjöberg exactly twenty-four hours after the jury had found him not guilty of criminal libel. That and his latest bout of celibacy had made the result certain. It would be impossible for Tillie to lose. Of course, it helped that Tillie had the best winning record of all women on the continent and that she was the most disciplined and serious. He didn't need those details in order to foresee her victory, but he couldn't deny that they were fortuitous.

Lisette was another matter. Petite, playful, charming, famous and French, Lisette brought something to Minneapolis that people had never seen before. She had raced all over Europe and was widely considered the fastest woman in the world. Haskell pushed her name in all the advertising, but it was hardly necessary: turning heads was easy for Lisette. Like Teddy Roosevelt, she could write her own headlines. Just support her with exaggerations and claims as if they were incontrovertible facts!

"Johnny Johnson says that Lisette is the fastest thing that breathes!"

Who is Johnny Johnson and when did he say it? Did he even say it? Would he deny saying it? Does it even matter?

Nah, Lisette is a safe bet.

IV

The press kept pushing Lisette's arrival like it was the onset of the entire Christmas season. But who she was, in fact, really depended on which paper you read.

In one account, she is a peasant girl tending sheep in a field in the Brittany countryside. A wealthy cycling enthusiast rides up to her and asks for directions. She is curious about his bicycle, and so he allows her to test it out. She loves it and rides off out of sight. She disappears for an entire hour. The wealthy man, overjoyed at her flirtatious playfulness and impressed with her natural aptitude, promises to return one day with a bicycle for her. A month later, he returns with the promised vehicle *and* an offer of marriage. With the support of her wealthy husband, Lisette begins her racing career.

In another account, Lisette is, again, a peasant girl. Country life is hard, and the girl is literally working herself to death in the fields. Her father takes her to the doctor who offers this very unexpected advice: "Buy this girl a bicycle and she will heal herself." Somehow, her peasant father finds the funds to buy a bicycle, which not only saves his daughter's life, but also enables her to become a racer.

In yet another account, Lisette is actually of royal blood, related directly to Prince Philippe, the Duke d'Orléans, himself. She has a strange and misplaced fascination with Napoléon Bonaparte. Her knowledge even surpasses that of all the best French historians. Before races, she answers all sorts of questions and even knows the finest details about French troop movements during the Battle of Austerlitz. Rumour spreads that her family of bluebloods strongly disapproves of her life choices. Napoleon scholar and *cyclienne*! Yes, her talent is beyond question, but how humiliating for her to glorify the Devil's favourite Corsican and to race for purses! After winning a race in Germany, The Duke d'Orléans allegedly commands her to return to Paris, an order which she, of course, ignores.

The final account, confirmed, somewhat, by vital statistics, begins with a peasant girl, removed from the fields of Brittany to work in a factory in Paris. She works there from the age of thirteen, and all the years working in the dark, dank conditions of the factory nearly kill her. Upstairs, an electrical engineer twenty years her senior hires a doctor to look into her health. The doctor confirms the man's fears: she will surely die unless she gets out of the factory. He marries the girl, now 19, and takes her to his home. But she is still ill and will not recover. The doctor returns, diagnoses the young woman with anaemia, and tells the husband, "Your wife will surely die if you do not return her to the countryside." They move. Her health improves a little, but not enough: her life is still under threat.

So, the doctor then prescribes exercise. Émile buys Lisette a bicycle, a children's bicycle, in fact, for even though she is now adult, she is still no larger than a child of twelve.

The bicycle heals her. She rides everywhere. Within two months she completes her first hundred-mile ride. It's amazing. She becomes a local celebrity—the young woman who rides everywhere on a child's bike. By 1894 she has already become the most celebrated woman cyclist in Paris.

These stories were so numerous and had such wide circulation that one acted like a brush hiding the tracks of the other. It didn't matter what was really being concealed or revealed. The audience loved all of it.

Usually, she was just Lisette, though sometimes she went by Lisette Marton. Her husband's name was Émile Christanet. Her real name seems to have been Amélie le Gall or le Gaul. The French press started calling her Lisette after she tested out a battery-powered bicycle at an electrical exposition. She was extremely small, less than five feet in height and weighing only eighty-five pounds. Her hundred-kilometre record was three hours and twenty-nine minutes, made on rough country roads. She completed one two-hour event with a sustained speed of nearly twenty-seven miles per hour. She finished her hour record with a distance of just under thirty miles. All these times put the American women to shame.

"I believe my greatest flaw is that I really don't care at all what others think of me," thought Lisette as she laughed out loud about her outfit. It had gotten her in trouble at the Royal Aquarium in London. The *Chronicle* reported that "the French girl's costume was sufficiently scanty to leave her legs free movement, and on this account she was subjected to some comment on the part of the English women who visited the Aquarium during the race." Lisette, in her usual matter-of-factness, dismissed the criticism. "When the men leave our races, what do they do? They go and applaud the *danseuses* on the stage who draw up their skirts to *cancan*. And they call us immodest because we wear a costume suitable to exertion on the wheel!? Hypocrisy!"

Lisette's arrival in Minneapolis was the subject of much attention from the press. The petite French racer sat up playfully and alert, speaking partially in English and partially with the aid of a translator.

"Yes, it's true. I would have died at the tender age of sixteen in that dreadful factory had I not met my husband and had he not bought me a bicycle. The instant I took the saddle, I recalled my childhood and how Lisette was always the first up the tree and always the first across the field and always the loudest to sing in church."

"So, the bicycle saved your life, Mlle. Lisette," stated one reporter.

Lisette's eyes sparkled.

10. Lisette

"My husband saved my life," she smiled. "He is my inspiration. I could not ride without him. He is as necessary as my cup of coffee." And then her blue eyes sparkled a little more. "You know I always have my cup of coffee, or else I could not know whether I am to win or lose the race." Lisette smiled and nodded significantly.

There was some hesitation and confusion in the journalists' gallery. Perhaps the translator made a mistake.

"Can you explain what you mean by that, Mlle. Lisette?"

"Really? But it's so simple…" She looked at the gallery of reporters incredulously for a moment, but then she leaned back in her chair and clapped her hands, giggling. "But what a stupid I am! I forget that everybody does not know the ways of Lisette. I drink my coffee in the morning. I always drink Turkish coffee, you know, not your American coffee, which the Italians call *acqua tinta*, and when I finish my coffee, I take it, turn it upside down, count to ten and then look inside. The coffee grinds leave trails and I read them. When I see many trails, I know that Lisette will make very much money. Just once I remember seeing no trails in my coffee. That was the day I lost to Mlle. Reillo. That Reillo makes my blood boil. I can never forget that. My husband said to me then that my heart was not in it, but he was wrong. It was the coffee. The hot, brown liquid decided. It is the coffee divination."

"And what did your coffee tell you this morning?"

"Today it was unclear. I saw many trails, but the trails had many branches. I have never seen anything like it before. I think it was suggesting that that Miss Anderson and Miss Farnsworth and the other ladies will not be so polite to Lisette during our six-day Festival of Fire race this week."

Someone in the press surmised that "many trails with many branches" was probably a good deal better than the usual "many trails." Another journalist, a correspondent from Boston, predicted that she was destined for greatness in Minneapolis, that she would "find her way into the Pantheon," even if she had got there by "riding on the backs of Pythian cattle." It didn't make a lot of sense, some hifalutin Massachusetts gibberish, but it sounded good. Bets were made accordingly.

V

First Night

Dovetailing the Ladies' Six-Day Race into the Festival of Fire was just like igniting a redemptive torch for all humanity to admire as it hastily and irrevocably separates the weak from the strong. It denuded any shred of sentimental pretense—the gamblers and the women were united, bound to the very idea of America's hastily won victory over the oceans of the world. The daytime traffic, which had witnessed the trophies, relics and re-enactments of war, would now rush into the main hall of the Industrial Exposition Building to watch the women fight it out. This is more than a competition for a mere prize; it is a re-enactment of—nay, something completely identical to—Washington's victory over Madrid.

There was no need to ever leave Minneapolis, at least not for a progressive, modern person. The State Fair in St. Paul was pointless. There can be no proud holler of the Thunderer in St. Paul tonight. They lost that scent when they dropped the voice of the forest into the bedpan. No, they all live ashore singing the hymn of the harvest, the same circle song they sing every single year. It's so damn old, but they act like it is a wellspring of life itself, when, in reality, it is just all toil without any glory: after all, they bring their wheat to us for grinding. No, it's all dried, worn hands in the cold, good earth over there. They keep dreaming of Acadia, as if in the gap between threshing and winnowing hid an emerald or a sapphire. Meanwhile, what is good is here, in Minneapolis.

A bike race there is not an emblem for anything and so the League of American Wheelmen (or the LAW, as it pompously refers to itself) excites the farmers with unharnessed mediocrity. Sure, the State Fair had its "Bicycle Day," but it was just shadow puppetry. To them, buried in dust and chaff, the bicycle is just the latest piece of newfangled metallurgy. They fancy their blacksmiths can forge the ball bearings, the yokels. And, you know what? They actually did hold men's races. They even enjoyed the endorsement of the LAW, but who could really be bothered to watch such nonsense? It was all just play-acting. Christ, it was as dull as Simple Simon—they couldn't even charge admission! Those men rode outdoors on an enormous, safe and boring half-mile track. Their prizes were puny—only thirty dollars for first prize. Their races were ridiculously short spurts—two miles was the longest event! No, forget the men at the State Fair. It's the women in Minneapolis who will do the real racing. Whoever wins the Ladies' Six-Day Race will leave with at least two hundred dollars, and she will have covered hundreds and hundreds of miles.

The State Fair won't even allow women to race. The LAW hates all ladies' racing. It even penalizes men who dare to compete against ladies. No, they corral the fair sex into competitions like "The Most Attractive Uniformed Club Composed Exclusively of Ladies," "The Lady Appearing in the Most Attractive and Best Bicycling Costume" and "The Most Graceful Lady Riding a Bicycle, Costume to be Considered." That's all they have for the ladies over in St. Paul. No, it's all old-fashioned and by the book over there. I mean, if you want to see horse racing, that's another matter. But if you want to see bicycle racing with the highest stakes and the hugest crowds and many, many feats and shining awestruck faces, you need to go no further than the Industrial Exposition Building at the Festival of Fire in Minneapolis. You can just forget about that horse and cabbage show in St. Paul.

The track stands in the Main Hall of the Exposition Building. The room is huge. It can easily accommodate the track, two bands and more than four thousand gambling spectators. Really, it is the best venue for an event like this. It already proved its worth when the Grand Old Party held its National Convention here in 1892. There is no question: we have the best place for the best race.

And it will be the best race. "Unless something unforeseen occurs," Haskell composed, "this will be the greatest *cyclienne* contest in the history of all racing annals. Records will go glimmering as old ones get shattered. The winner will be, in very truth, and beyond all dispute, the champion *cyclienne* of the world."

The gambling prospects are sure to blow up. Tens of thousands of dollars will change hands. Yes, the gamblers will converge on Minneapolis. Believing they are the heroes at the climax of a most fortuitous adventure, they will place their bets. A wager, they always claim, is an expression of personal agency. The ladies—their training, their effort, their desires, their risks—are incidental. The wager is everything. Longing is knowledge and foresight. No one loses, ever, because losing is impossible. My wallet will look like an overstuffed cabbage roll; my neighbour's will look like a pitted prune. My bet will cross the finish line victorious and unscathed; let the others pass through the meat-grinder, for all I care.

The first night, every seat was filled. Fully four thousand people witnessed. The bands played John Philip Sousa all night long, "Semper Fidelis," "The Rifle Regiment March," "Hands across the Sea," "The Thunderer" and others. These tireless marches complemented the patriotic and progressive purpose of the Festival of Fire and fanned the sentiments of the crowd. But one song stood out as unusual. Again and again, the band played "King Cotton." Why? William Haskell smiled each time it played. King Cotton was the nickname of J. Robertson Smiley, the President of the Cycling Carnival Company and the man who had made the entire event a reality. Who knows why they call him King Cotton? Who cares? Smiley is smiling: that is all that matters.

Suddenly, the band stopped playing. There was a pause of silence as the audience settled. The master of ceremonies introduced the riders as they walked out one-by-one. There was cheering for each racer, but when Lisette came out, the crowd went berserk. The master of ceremonies asked everyone to settle down, and then he announced that it was time to play the "Star Spangled Banner." All rose, the anthem played, and all sat down. Then a giant gong splashed, and the racers began their two hours of racing for the evening.

As a welcome gesture to the French guest, Lisette was given post of vantage on the inside. Farnsworth took next spot, followed by Anderson, Williams, Peterson and Drehmel. Lisette smiled playfully, her eyes sparkling. It was so kind to give her the inside lane. She waved and blew kisses to the audience. Meanwhile, the other racers were completely focused on the start. The trainers held their bicycles for them as they clipped their shoes into their pedals.

Dottie Farnsworth had been collecting newspaper clippings about Lisette all week long. Now that she was shoulder-to-shoulder with the petite Frenchie, she was starting to panic. How could someone so small have a reputation so large? How could she ride so fast? Lisette turned to face Dottie and gave her a warm smile. Dottie smirked. Lisette might get the inside lane at the start, but that is the only concession she was going to get. She must not get ahead, not even by the width of one spindly spoke.

Tillie tried not to notice Lisette. That smile was charming, admittedly, but this was no place for charm. How stupid and dishonest. Tillie looked at the track under her front wheel, she looked at her pedals and then at her handlebars. She even looked up into the roaring crowd for a moment. Despite these efforts, eventually Tillie looked again at Lisette. The French woman then smiled even more, and she actually started to giggle. She looked like an imbecile. Who does this at the starting line? It must be cunning, an attempt to unhinge her main rival. Tillie looked down at the track to regain focus. Ridiculous. Let spinning wheels decide who gets to smile at the finish.

"Now, darling, take it easy. This is the first night. We don't need to overdo it," said Phil gently into Tillie's ear. He spoke in Swedish so the others couldn't understand.

She ignored him. He was just trying to comfort himself. Thank goodness he never heard her questions about wheels and finish lines.

"No need to go the whole hog," he added in English.

Dottie's ears perked up. She leaned back in her saddle, looked at Tillie and smirked. Tillie ignored her, but Phil made eye contact with her and pursed his lips under his mustache. It was stupid to give away anything for free.

The night's result would be decided by two separate processes. In one corner, the power to call the finish was left in the able hands of the grand clock above the track. In the other, the women would decide, measuring out the evening in breakaways, elbow jabs, near misses and crashes. These actions would culminate in a certain number of laps. To the winner, these two processes would appear united; to everyone else, it would feel like one was resisting the other.

But, in the meantime, how can the race be summarized? It was the first of six days of racing. There were plenty of efforts at breakaways. There was a lot of "Dottie took off with the power of a river" and "Lisette spurted ahead to take the lead." Lillie Williams held everyone off for an astounding twenty laps. Even Clara Drehmel had a few minutes of glory: she took the lead and temporarily transubstantiated from "The German" back into a "Minneapolis girl." Other than these little moments of glory, the night consisted mostly of Lisette charming the crowd, Farnsworth, Williams and Peterson blocking Lisette, and, of course, Anderson absolutely dominating everything.

But the main takeaway from the first night was that Lisette crashed. She had not even completed four miles when it happened. Tillie had unsettled the group with an early and angry sprint. Lisette lost control in the scramble and fell hard.

Tillie looked over her shoulder as the crash took place, and she saw Lisette smile as she flew down, hip first, straight to the floor. By the time Tillie did one circle, Lisette was still on the track, lying face down, convulsing. Was she crying? Tillie locked eyes on Lisette and caught a glimpse of her face as she rolled past fast: she was laughing heartily and joyfully. What a strange girl.

But Lisette's countenance had completely changed when she got up. No longer smiling, she grimaced, held her arm out and turned imploringly to the crowd: look what the Terrible Swede did to me, she seemed to say. What a bad girl that Tillie Anderson is! How could she do this to me?

That faker! She sure put on a pitiful face as her husband helped her back on her bicycle. She, who had just been cackling maniacally into the boards not a minute ago. What a show! Wincing every time her left leg was fully extended, and curling crookedly over her handlebars like a hunchback. What a performance!

"Look at that Lisette. She sure has some pluck, that one."

"To carry on through the pain like that, not everyone can do that, you know."

"That Anderson is too rough, always scaring the other girls with her mad dashes!"

When Tillie won the first night, she thought about the Father of the Waters again. Obviously, it was a stupid image, but it was just an idea, a comparison. It is true that the river is strong, much stronger than a man. It is tireless and godlike. You can harness that power to grind up flour and saw wood, but who would claim to be able to channel that strength into a racer? What would that even mean, to have the power of the river and to race? Isn't that power better suited to some other purpose?

There was no conclusion to such thoughts. At least they took attention away from Lisette's accusations, which would brew and froth and bubble in the spectators' minds as they slept that night.

VI
Second Night

Again, Sousa's marches played on, again, the clocked would count two hours, again, Lisette smiled warmly at the crowd and giggled at the starting line, and, again, Tillie was silent and thoughtful.

The only difference was Farnsworth. She donned a dashing red suit and draped the Stars and Stripes on her shoulders like a cape. She walked up to her bicycle with a commanding gait, grabbed the handlebars heroically and straddled her saddle with her long, red leg, which she brandished like a mill wheel. (The men in the audience sat a little straighter in their seats to follow this motion). Dottie looked at Lisette and sniffed. She then ceremoniously handed the flag to her assistant, who fumbled it because he was also supporting her on her bicycle.

In the papers—not in *The Minneapolis Times*—there had been some discussion about the track. Was it safe? Many remarked that it did not have high enough barriers at the corners. If speeds got too high, wouldn't the ladies fly off? That is not quite what happened, though the morning's musings in the press did get one thing right: the second night would end in calamity.

As her little show with the flag and red outfit implied, Dottie had plans, and right from the gong splash it became clear that Lisette figured prominently in them. Before the first turn, she was already barricading the French champion. Lisette made repeated attempts to pass, but Dottie always shot out an elbow to block her way. Peterson and Williams saw this strategy and liked it. They started copying Dottie, and so it happened that three women teamed up on the little French guest whose name had head-lined every Fire Festival advertisement since June.

Tillie didn't want to get involved. Really, you might as well openly profess your fear and jealousy. Why advertise weakness? There were those silly ads that promised to restore manhood, nerve seeds, cupidine, sana-tivo and the like. Dottie and the others needed something like that, not to restore "manhood," obviously. This was not a matter of "youthful errors" surrounding the "generative organs." But, clearly, they needed to restore something. It was impossible to ride like that and look in the mirror in the morning. No, it wasn't necessary to help Lisette, but nor would it do any good to get involved with all the jockeying and blocking. If there is more to this than wheels and finish lines, then there is no need for cheating.

The obstructions and barricades continued all night. With each thwarted attempt to pass, Lisette shrugged her shoulders and made a broad, incredulous face, rolling back briefly out of the scrum to make com-mentary on it. No one could hear her. They wouldn't have understood her French in any case. Nevertheless, the audience knew exactly what she was complaining about. Dottie was a menace.

Before you knew it, thousands of patriotic Americans celebrating for patriotic purpose had turned against the All-American Dottie and started rooting for the French visitor. Dottie would not have been so horrified had she recalled just how much money had been bet on Lisette. But it was impossible to acknowledge this. It was impossible to believe that coffee divination and charisma could prove to be so much stronger than national sentiment. And yet, there it was: and so Dottie was twisted into a distressed and agitated state without completely understanding why.

Tillie, fed up with the blocking, took the lead. Phil had forgotten to whistle, but she didn't need him. She knew there was just a minute left. Time to tear across lots and win. She stood out of the saddle and jumped on her pedals with all her might. She entered the high turn, climbing the berm so she could descend out of it on her exit, using gravity to pull her ahead of the others. It was her favorite move.

And Dottie knew it. She saw it coming and made to follow Tillie up the bank, but she also insisted on blocking Lisette, who was also hoping to snap after Tillie's sprint. Distressed, confused, angry and desperate, Dottie misjudged and went too high. The protective barrier, low and useless down by her shins, startled her. She flinched, her front wheel went out from under her, and she fell across the track. Lisette was right behind, and before anyone realized what had happened, she rode right over Dottie's leg. Lisette's wheel threw her, and she landed with a thud on the hard track. Peterson came next, and she crashed straight into the pair and was thrown down too. Tillie flew ahead as the others tumbled behind her. Williams and Drehmel had already left the track to make room for the final sprint, so they entirely avoided the scramble.

Tillie kept riding until she had to stop: a crowd had flooded onto the track to help the fallen competitors. Peterson was not badly hurt. She was helped to her feet and escorted to her dressing room. Lisette and Dottie were knocked out cold.

Farnsworth regained consciousness first. Her moans were pitiful to hear: "She rode straight over me like a dog in the street. I think she broke my leg!"

Dottie's mother stormed through the crowd: "Oh, this is terrible," she exclaimed. "I'll never let her go on the track again."

Lisette lay motionless for a long time. Many looked on in fear and waited. Did we kill her? When she finally came to her senses, there were great sighs of relief and then a grand applause. She sat on the track as her husband Émile bandaged a great bruise on her forehead, a giant gouge on her left arm at the elbow and cuts too numerous to count on her hips and arms. After the dressings were done, Émile carried his tiny wife slowly out of the Exhibition Building. The crowd looked on as she bore the pain without a single cry or word of complaint. Journalists followed her to her carriage and would chase her back to her hotel to stay with her late into the night to get the story for the morning paper.

As for Dottie, they were certain her leg was broken. They attempted to carry her, but she writhed and hollered with pain. They left her lying in the middle of the track until she regained her composure. Lisette had already left the building by the time they finally carried Dottie to her dressing room.

Tillie was hiding in the staircase, deep in thought.

A race used to feel like a fight—a fight against gravity, wind resistance and the likes of Lisette, Dottie and all the other women. This rivalry hinged on speed, on strength, on skill, on endurance and on toughness. It was all contained within lines, ending with the crossing of that final finish line. It didn't feel that way anymore, or it felt wrong to look at it that way. It was impossible to explain why.

A champion might win so many races that she forgets who she is. She becomes the race; then, who is she and where did she go?

There was that story about the *bortbyting*, the *changeling*, from her grandmother's fairy tales back in Sweden: the trolls take a baby girl from her crib and replace her with their own monstrous child. Simple country folk, the parents don't even notice. The girl is brought up with trolls and the troll is brought up in the village.

This might be more than just a fairy tale. A person might live a life in one way, only to discover later that that life had not been hers to live, or that she had somehow been robbed of the life she was supposed to live. But, surely, if a person concluded she were a changeling, she would also have to be ill. Is that what these past few months have been? An illness? It seemed unlikely. And yet it is not normal to ruthlessly cast away years of life and hard work...

What had once just been an arena with rules now appeared to be a circus to beat all circuses. And it was all so... small-minded. Everyone pulled together to pull the wool over each other's eyes. Everyone hoodwinked each other and everyone happily submitted to each other's deceptions. It was a weird game that played at being not a game, where all the rules were just subterfuges concealing deeper rules. Everyone fought, but, in fighting, they were really pulling together. What were they all pulling? Where were they pulling it to? Why help to pull when you can't answer these sorts of questions?

Am I the human baby, thrust into the realm of the rock trolls? Or am I the *bortbyting*, the little baby troll secretly dropped into the peasant mother's crib? Despite this line of questions—or perhaps because of it—there was something familiar, like a ghost coming back to haunt itself.

The dangerous track, Dottie's unfairness, Lisette's feigned fatalism and charisma, the roaring and gambling crowd and her lingering anger about

Reverend Moody and Fanny Darling—it all built up. What had once seemed like the testing site of personal merit now looked like a circus, and she was just another one of the acts. Tillie didn't know if she wanted to go on.

Phil found Tillie on the stairs. It did not look good. True, she was in first place, but how unusual for her to stare off so vacantly into space, like someone vanquished. How on earth had she avoid Lisette and Dottie's pile-up? How had she translated that danger into victory when she was so distracted? She needed to snap out of it.

"Tillie, darling," said Phil. "If you could only focus, things would be so much more… certain."

She looked at him like he was a fly buzzing around her head.

"If you are able to ride this well when you're in such a state, just imagine what you could do with your head in the game." He smiled despite her frown, "I know you'll do what's right."

She could have smacked him, and she actually wound up in order to do so.

That was exactly the moment when Officer Chamberlain shook her roughly by the shoulder. He wanted to clear the staircase to make room for the men carrying Dottie out of the building.

"Move aside, miss."

Tillie turned to face him, hand drawn to swing and daggers in her eyes. Chamberlain knew that look and that pose. He assumed they were aimed at him, so then he added, "…please, Miss Anderson. Move aside, please."

The *Minneapolis Times* told quite a different version of this story. Tillie clenched her fist and threw not one but two punches "with all her force," right into Officer Chamberlain's nose. It alleged that half a dozen policemen rushed to the spot to stop Tillie's assault. "One of the guardians of the peace volunteered the opinion that Tillie was no lady."

VII
Third Night

Had Tillie actually punched a police officer or not? No one cared. Lisette had seized everyone's attention with an even better story.

11. Tillie Anderson

"I will not let them trick me," Lisette told the reporters in her hotel room late that evening. She sat up straight, bandages all over her head, arms and legs.

In this way, a series of accusations appeared in the morning's paper and set a new tone for the rest of the race. Lisette alleged that not only was Dottie Farnsworth deliberately blocking her attempts to pass (which was entirely true), but that Tillie Anderson had hired Lillie Williams to block and jockey her as well (which was a deliberately told lie). It was outrageous. But then people recalled how Lisette had predicted precisely this sort of thing in her coffee reading before the race. Her prediction had come true. She said it before the race and she's saying it now. Coffee divination was real.

When the five thousand spectators showed up for the race that evening, they were all on Lisette's side. The moment the gallant little Parisienne appeared from her dressing room, the entire crowd roared its approval. It was so loud that the bands had to stop playing.

Gambling that night reflected public sentiment precisely.

Lisette sheepishly dragged her damaged bicycle behind her. She had snapped a crank in the previous night's crash. Appealing to her Minneapolitan hosts for help, she hoped another set of wheels would materialize. Somehow another bicycle was procured for her. No one really understood how or who donated it. Yes, it was a little too large for her, and she wouldn't be able to use her sponsor's chain, but she rode a couple of warm-up laps to assess, declared the wheel adequate to her needs, and agreed to continue to race. The applause was grand.

Dottie was also at the start. She had recovered from her crash completely, it seemed, though she was dressed a good deal more modestly. As the night progressed, she did not block Lisette, not even once. She kept her elbows to herself and gave her French rival plenty of space. No need risking another crash.

But now it was Lillie Williams who picked up where Dottie had left off. She mercilessly blocked Lisette every chance she got. The crowd hissed wildly, but Lillie just scoffed. Finally, a referee gave her a warning. Public opinion held that Lillie was discriminating against Lisette, and that it probably was true that Tillie had hired her to do this. Phil Sjöberg objected, "There is no such discrimination. Why would Miss Anderson hire help? She is perfectly capable of winning on her own." But there were murmurs against Tillie. Mr. Sjöberg's denial only made his wife seem more suspicious.

With an alien bicycle, her injuries and all of Lillie's blocking, Lisette finished fourth that night. But when she left her dressing room later that evening to go to her carriage she was hailed by a burst of cheering. Women, who had waited an hour in the chill of a September night, rushed up to her and grasped her hands, pouring out words of congratulations and friendship.

Lisette replied with a bright smile, "*Je vous aime aussi!*"*

VIII
Fourth Night

The fourth night of the race was as fair as could be wished...until the last mile. Anderson set the tone with a big sprint. Ever on guard to catch the scent, Lisette jumped on her pedals in pursuit. But she had to eat her way through Dottie and Lillie to catch Tillie's wheel. Lillie took the night off and let Lisette pass without a struggle, but the fighting spirit had returned to Dottie. She shot out her elbow and tilted her rump to make the pass as difficult as possible. And it worked. Tillie won, with Dottie in second and Lisette in third.

Lisette was furious. She demanded the referees call a foul.

"*Farnsworth a fait comme ça!*"† she complained, copying the elbow motion that had vexed her all week long. "*C'est toujours comme ça.*"‡ Dottie had to be stopped, and, if the referees wouldn't do it, then Lisette would take matters into her own hands, and she angrily shook her fist.

One referee agreed that Dottie had deliberately blocked Lisette. But another referee took Dottie's side: it was Lisette who had fouled the

---

* "I love you too."

† "Farnsworth did this!"

‡ "It's always like that."

American woman. The third referee settled the matter: he hadn't seen anything. The women kept their original finishing positions.

Taking Lisette's threat of retribution seriously, it was thought that Dottie should leave the track first. The Minneapolis native was still suffering from her injuries of the second night. She stumbled off her bike and winced. She hobbled off the track. The audience booed and hissed after her. The band even played a quick, mocking tune to accompany her exit, much to the audience's great pleasure.

The crowd saw Lisette off with its usual gushing fanfare, but there was some quiet grumbling. It was now impossible for Lisette to win the six-day race. The best she could hope for was third place overall. Coffee had foreseen the challenge of Farnsworth and Anderson; the gamblers should have foreseen how those challenges would impact the final results. It was a brutal realization. Unless she had a horrible crash, there was no way Tillie could lose.

To Tillie, this insight made her feel a little nauseous. To race, to be winning—she was beginning to take an ironic view on these matters. But to be threatened with the possibility of a fix, especially one of a violent nature, was disturbing. And if there wasn't a fix, the fact she would win without even trying made the whole matter absurd.

To ride instead of stitching, to make a lot of money instead of scraping by to make ends meet in a Chicago apartment—these were things she enjoyed about her life and how racing had changed it. But she had already accomplished that. What next? What did it really mean to race? Coming in first? No, that can't be all! But how can you go further than victory?

And why is Dottie happy to keep on blocking Lisette? And why is Lisette happy to keep on … crashing? What is she hoping to accomplish? And why is she always lying and laughing and crying?

IX
Fifth Night

Lillie Williams, no longer a contender for the win, decided her performance tonight needed something extra. She wore a white racing suit with black hose. A giant sailor-style collar topped her sweater and a giant American flag sashed around her waist. *The Minneapolis Times* remarked that "the Omaha girl certainly made a fetching appearance."

Dottie felt upstaged: "You know you were supposed to wear the other flag," she whispered into Lillie's ear.

"I guess I'm just being myself," Lillie said and kept looking ahead.

Lillie's outfit had ignited something within her. The audience loved the get up, and, for once, she was getting the cheers and adulation, not Lisette. The difference in her riding was unmistakable. Lillie set the pace more than any other rider that evening. Out in front, taking the pulls, she even imagined that she was dominating Tillie, who was, it seemed, holding back. Towards the end of the night, it was as if something were calling out to Lillie. She had already worked so hard. Now was the time to set up a tremendous effort and try to take the whole night. Get some glory. She couldn't win the six-day race anymore, but at least she could take the fifth night.

She climbed out of her saddle, imagined her legs were the pistons of a locomotive, and set her head down to do some very heavy work. The crowd immediately recognized her body language. Its cheers swelled over the banks and pooled into the track like a flood. Lisette, Tillie and Peterson jumped onto her attack with all their might. Dottie and Clara, spent, had nothing left to give and fell back to make room for the others to make their final sprint.

Lillie made it through the turn when her front wheel suddenly slipped. She flew into the track. Lisette, Peterson and Tillie were right behind her, and they all went down in the wreck. The women lay in the middle of the track, a tangle of soldiers, crumpled and beaten, in a wide and dry wood-grain trench.

Lillie was lucky. She had only landed on her knee, and the women behind her had crashed into her bike, not her. She was fine. Still, she lay there, angry and regretful. This was not how the evening was supposed to end.

Tillie knew she was all right. She landed on her hip with all her weight. It was very painful, but, as far as she could tell, she was unharmed. She just lay there on the track in the fetal position, with her eyes closed.

After a few moments, she opened her eyes.

There, inches away, was Lisette's bruised and scuffed up face. She looked horrible. Her hair was tangled, her left eye was swollen, she still had the bandage on her head from three nights ago, and now she had a friction burn on her right cheek too. Her eyes were still closed because she was frowning, almost in tears. "*Assez*,"* she said aloud, shaking her puffy, gauzy head.

Then she opened her eyes and it was like Christmas morning. Lisette was the first to offer a smile. It spread playfully across her face. Tillie started to smile back, and then Lisette started to giggle. It was difficult not to laugh. It was so remarkable—silly, really. Lisette grabbed Tillie's hand and squeezed it excitedly and lovingly. The two women briefly held hands, smiling and trying not to laugh, lying on their sides in the middle of the track.

Phil came running. He saw his wife and her rival, shook his head, and then he picked Tillie up and dragged her away from the strange little French girl.

Tillie looked at the smiling Lisette, who was still lying in the track, playfully propping her head on her hand and waving goodbye. Tillie smiled back, but then suddenly thought of Dottie thundering around the turn: "Clear her off the track, boys!" she hollered at the trainers.

X

Sixth Night

The bands made room for the newsboys to play on the final night. Sentimental tunes scraped out of clarinets and a cornucopia of brass tubes to the accompaniment of a giant bass drum and a snare. This was William Edwin Haskell's foray into philanthropy. Teach the newsboys to play an instrument. Get them out in front of a crowd to play. It's good for everyone. Or, at least it looks good. Good enough.

After six days, the final result was not a surprise: Tillie won, Dottie came in second and Lisette got third. The bookies tried to soften the blow by emphasizing how, finally, Lisette beat Dottie on the sixth night. The

---

* "enough"

overall standings were one thing, but the sixth night was another. Lisette beat Dottie, for once; nothing else mattered.

William Haskell gambled everything on Tillie and won a lot of money. His acquaintances were quite surprised, having expected him to wager the way he had encouraged them to do. No matter. He was quick to rally his connections at the Chamber of Commerce and to arrange for Lisette to have more races. The French Dynamo had proven herself, and Minneapolis's leading men, with Haskell at the helm, formed a pool of money to back her against any living rider in a hundred-mile race on any track. Lisette was happy to oblige. She would not be returning to France any time soon.

Tillie seemed to be riding confidently. It didn't matter anymore. She had had a crash, as she had anticipated. It was serious enough, but apparently not catastrophic. It certainly was not deliberate. Her mind wandered onto other things.

This track, you could divide it all up into sixteenth-inch sectors. You could fight for every single sixteenth inch, care intensely about owning the sector at the front, how many sectors behind, measure, down to the finest micronewton, how much energy your opponents would need to catch you, and then adjust your effort with the difference. You conquer as many of these fractions of inches as you are able before time runs out. The others will curse when you beat them, but, in the end, they are only shaking their fists over an accumulation of miniscule measurements. In this way, we turn each race into a battle over sixteenth inches.

Or, you can see the track as one place. It's still a collection of sixteenth inches, but now the difference between one and the other is irrelevant. One sixteenth of an inch is exactly the same as 368 miles. It might as well be infinity. The track is still a centrifuge, but the spinning now has a different meaning: whereas before there was the dizziness of frenzied exertion, exhaustion and anxiety over who would win, now there was another type of dizziness, reminiscent of that feeling you had whenever you rolled down a grassy hill with your sister.

The track is still a testing ground, but no longer are we testing for victory, for dominance, or to see who finishes first. It isn't clear what we are testing. It has something to do with Lisette's smile—a smile that can still be conjured despite a black eye and the possibility of a ruptured spleen. It also has to do, somehow, with again finding Lisette's extended and glad hand.

XI

Tillie and Phil took the carriage from the Exposition Building to their hotel. They had tucked out early. Tillie had nothing to say to the press.

"Take us on a scenic route, please, driver," Tillie requested.

The driver took the Hennepin Bridge, just up river from St. Anthony's Falls. Tillie noticed the roaring water for the first time. Under a full moon, she could see the current sparkle and the light mist rise. The Father of the Waters lived here. He had been presiding over the race all along, perpetually falling, churning. She looked up and down the river at all the gristmills—chalky blue shadows vying for space on the riverside in order to dip their wheels into the water so they could grind wheat into flour.

As they crossed, the driver looked over at Nicollet Island. He had been born there among the maples. They said it was 1862, probably one of the last children to be born there. And the people used to gather syrup there, before the land was sold. His mother had taught him they used to call St. Anthony's Falls a *long song*, a *voice inside a whirlpool and underneath the giant, splintered rocks.*

"My mother told me the falls were a place of games of fear and make-believe. 'We danced on the edge,' she said. 'We didn't speak,' she said. 'And not speaking we hid our eyes from each other, pretending to be wolves, but wolves from different packs. And after the game was done,' she told me, 'we laughed and hugged. The make-believe allowed us to see the end and to keep it away for as long as possible—we knew it was coming,' she said. 'But when the game was over and the future died, we just loved each other all the more. We knew we had just a little more time, but we knew we had the time we had.' At least, so she said."

Tillie was nodding off, but she liked her driver's voice. It was nice to hear a different way of speaking—a gentle man with a gentle voice. Carried on the calm clip-clopping of the horse's hooves and the sound of falling water, this man's voice sounded like a lullaby.

But games of vertigo and mimicry? What on earth was he talking about? She roused herself to ask the strange, gentle man a question. She was thinking about the Father of the Waters again.

"All these mills, how long did it take to build them?"

"I dunno, Ma'am. But I can tell you that they still build more. The river ain't big enough for all the mills they aim to build here. They grind so much flour here that there was this one time when it all exploded and nearly destroyed the place. The exploding flour tore up buildings and killed people. They say they could feel the earth shake all the way in St. Paul. It was awful!

"Yes, Ma'am, they're crazy with mills here in Minneapolis. In fact, Ma'am, they built so many mills here that they finally killed the falls. Make no mistake, those falls you hear now are false. The true ones, the ones where my mother says they used to dance, they collapsed. Too much building. Too many channels. Too many tunnels. They dug right under the falls. They aimed to reach a tunnel to this island we're on here. But the falls—the *long song*—it didn't like what they were doing and it said it had enough. They collapsed. It was horrible. I was just a boy. I remember it like it was yesterday."

"But that can't be right?"

"How's that?"

"Well, I can hear falls. I can see the mist."

"Well, they were really afraid. They thought Minneapolis was done. They asked the President to make new falls, and that's what they went and done. Soldiers come and built it. What you hear now is the army's falls, not my mother's. To build it, they had to kill the voice in the water, at least the one my mother says they used to dance to. Now it's just water pouring over a skirt of concrete. No, the voice inside the whirlpool and underneath the giant, splintered rocks is dead. It ain't never coming back neither."

CHAPTER THREE

The Mikhailovskii Manège

St. Petersburg, Russia, January and February 1897

I

With a well-worn gesture, the young correspondent twirled his mustache and smiled. "Does Mlle. Reillo have any words to convey to her readers at *Paris-Vélo*?"

Victorine Reillo, bruised and stitched, smiled with gently pleading discouragement as she lay propped in bed in a suite of the Hôtel de l'Hérmitage. The bed was a monument to her recovery, a lovely throne of homespun linen, where she had to remain until her stitches healed and her bandages could be removed. Meanwhile all the other French racers, Étéogella, Tual, Lamberjack, all of them, would be returning to Paris, in time for the spring. Lucky devils. Victorine would be staying behind in Russia for the rest of the winter.

Even though Victorine had arrived in St. Petersburg by train almost a month ago, she still had not figured out what the date was. Her attention was so keenly focused on the races and now on her injuries that she had lost count. The Russian calendar measured the days just as well as the one back home, only it was late, just like that acquaintance who never arrives on time, whose friends have to invent some fib to impose punctuality upon him. Victorine couldn't figure out the trick to decoding this calendar, and so she always felt uncertain; it being February only made matters worse.

"Could you tell me, if you please, what is the date today? I mean in Paris, of course."

"Damned if I know," guffawed the correspondent. "Time here has turned my head around completely. All I know is that the train station is just down the way and that I leave tonight."

Whatever the date was, it must have been about fortnight's remove from her comprehension. Was she being tugged backwards through time, or was it she who was pulling the Russian Empire ahead into the future? Who could say? All she knew was this: it was certainly Saturday, her compatriots had apparently already returned to France without saying goodbye, she was bedridden with the worst injuries of her life and she was trapped in St. Petersburg for the foreseeable future. Worst of all, it was winter. The days were as dark as treacle.

"Does Mlle. Reillo expect to be comfortable during her convalescence in St. Petersburg?"

"I am certain the prince has thought of everything. He has proven better than his word in every respect. Frankly, we racers have never had a better host."

"Well, Mlle. Reillo, I'm sure I speak for all our readers at *Paris-Vélo* when I declare my sincerest wishes for your complete and rapid recovery. Racing in France simply will not be the same without you."

"Thank you. You are too kind."

"Truly, your presence will be sorely missed."

Victorine pressed her hands gently to her chest, feigning a gracious nod and smile. Yes, having the support of the press was wonderful, but, really, the young man's behaviour was becoming burdensome. He had tried bragging about his promotion to correspondent after serving as the paper's advertising solicitor for far too long; when that didn't work he resorted to these heavy sighs and insinuations. What a pathetic little so-and-so. There's the door. What's the hold up?

12. Victorine Reillo in 1897

The newspapers were the *cyclienne*'s scripture—they built her up out of nothing; but they never built you up as high as you deserved. For every time you were called *"Reillo la championne du kilometre,"* *"Reillo, la meilleure des dames"* or *"Reillo la up-and-comer,"* you were also called *"la gentille Reillo,"* *"l'amiable Reillo,"* *"la petite Reillo"** or even *"Reillo l'exquise"* with *"un minois séduisant."*† One time someone had called her *"une lionne."* That was more or less accurate. Just add *furieuse. La lionne furieuse.* Yes, that would be perfect.

But no one ever went so far. They watch this beast named Victory reach for the win every single time she gets on the track, never relenting, and the best you can do is talk about a pretty face? Fools, say what you like. One day you'll see: little by little the bird builds its nest.

II

As the correspondent was leaving and making one, final and especially meaningful nod to Victorine, Gabby stormed through the doorway. She dwarfed the young man with hawkish and impetuous movements. It had seemed, for a while there, that perhaps Gabby would just leave without a word. But no, she came after all. That bitch never missed an opportunity. Besides, they had made a bet.

"Well, look what we have here," said Gabrielle, shaking her head, smiling scornfully as she looked around the hotel room. "When the beast dies, its venom dies too! Though, perhaps that is a little rich in your case. But how did you allow this to happen to you, Vi-Vi?"

"Why don't you come a little closer, Gabby, and I'll show you."

"Thank you, *non, lavette,*‡" chuckled Gabrielle. "It is much more comfortable over here, on my feet." Gabrielle lifted a leg and placed it on the chair beside her, leaning forward as she pulled out an enormous wad of rubles from her coat. The bills looked dazzling, motley and gargantuan compared to francs and pounds. "Again, we see that I am *la championne* and you are my *domestique*, hmm? And you were hoping to put me in my

---

* "Reillo the kind," "Reillo the amicable," "Reillo the small"

† "Reillo the exquisite" with "a seductive little face"

‡ *literally* "dishcloth," but it means "wimp"

place. Not this time, not last time, not ever, *ma chérie. Non.*" She held out her other hand and said, "You know what I came for…"

Victorine winced from the pain as she reached to pull out a small reticule tied around her neck. It bulged out like a man's fist and felt like an overripe banana peel. She tore out a clump of rubles, every single one she had earned in St. Petersburg that winter, and flung the money at Gabrielle who caught all the bills across her chest just as they started to scatter.

Gabrielle grinned with all her front teeth as she counted the bills and added them to her stack: "Ah, yes! Good wine does not need a cork."

"There is no cork that could possibly plug you, Gabby."

Gabrielle had not expected that: "What's that supposed to mean?"

"You know what I mean. I know you needed my sacrifice, but …" It was too embarrassing to say the rest out loud. Gabrielle's coupling of bitchiness and blindness used to arouse generous pity; today it appeared shameful.

"How's that? … Bah, whatever!" snorted Gabrielle. "*Dommage, ma chérie.* A good appetite is worth more than a good meal." And the spiteful woman pulled out a pink jersey and thrust it in a heap upon Victorine's lap. "I cannot take that with me. It was intended for you all along." Gabrielle looked into Victorine's eyes, searchingly, questioningly, for the first time in months: "Well, may you not die here, Vi-Vi! It would be a shame to perish here *une veille fille** in this icy, dark wasteland. You'd deprive the world of a great beauty! On the other hand, maybe you will become a Russian princess, *non?*"

Victorine made no comment.

"I guess you could do a lot worse, Vi-Vi," laughed Gabrielle. "The lad was obviously born with heavy pockets. And a prince is still a prince, after all. But if at any time you want to make a run for it, Vi-Vi, the train station is just a few steps away. *Adieu!*"

With that, Gabrielle Étéogella stormed towards the door, laughing; just before exiting, she stopped and pointed at a painting on the wall, looked back at Victorine incredulously and added, "Can you believe that?"

And with those words, Gabrielle Étéogella laughed and exited the room. Off she went to Paris.

---

* *literally* "an old girl," a euphemism for spinster

III

A silence hung over the unbelievable room: everything was elegant, open and tidy—the carpets, the wallpaper, the fixtures, the enormous windows, the high ceiling and the white porcelain-tiled stove. The linen, wrapped neatly and tightly around her legs and torso, was absolutely alien: touching it made one feel embarrassed to have lived so long without having touched it before. On the wall facing her bed was an enormous mirror with an elegant floral frame. The leaves and petals carved from hardwood made a petrified dance around the looking glass, so that the frame almost consumed the reflection it contained. On the other wall, next to the door, hung a painting of a group of men standing around a bull. The men held daggers, and their faces were buttery with lifted, questioning brows. Meanwhile, the sacrificial bull confronted these clerics with a resolute and stony face. That was what Gabby had gawked at and mocked on her way out the door. It was an incomprehensible image. Good thing Prince *comment s'appele** was paying for all this.

Adjusting the pillow was too painful. Shifting to the other side was too painful. Pulling the blankets was too painful. The morphia was starting to wear off. The young man had said the train station is just a few steps away. Gabby said the same... Might as well be on the other side of the Russian Empire.

All this because of that hag-fairy Marie Tual. What was her problem? All month long she had been hiding behind everyone, waiting, and for what? Then she wakes up in the final lap of the final race, sneaks out of nowhere, falls on that damned near impossible turn, eats Victorine's wheel and sends her crashing hard. It was an atrocious crash, too, as if a god had tried to polish and buff the track with Victorine's body, but he was too powerful to notice—or to care—that her body was still all tangled up in her bicycle.

No, Tual had ruined everything. Why couldn't she have taken out Gabby's wheel instead? Gabrielle was the dragon, the long, dreadful and wrathful serpent, bathing in her own venom. She should be the one

---

* "Prince what's his name"

strapped and trapped in Russia. Lord knows she deserved it. That interview she gave last October filled the cup of Victorine's patience over the brim:

"How much are your winnings so far this season?"

"Oh brother, I really cannot recall. Who cares? I win so much that I never want for anything anyway."

"That must be nice!"

"Oh, trust me, it is! Yes, I'm—as they say—happy as a king, or, in this case, as a queen!"

"And, Queen Étéogella, in your entire career so far, what is your most cherished memory?"

"Oh, that's easy! It would have to be all the times I defeated Reillo. Yeah, I guess beating those English girls at the Agricultural Hall was pretty good too, but, yeah, mostly Reillo. Defeating her is always cause for celebration."

"Lately it has been happening a lot, seems."

"There's no such thing as a *fête* that can't last until tomorrow. At least, I've never seen one."

Defeating Gabrielle had transmogrified into a gargantuan blazing torch in the long, desolate night of failure. Only to beat her! Then life would start anew. All the failures of the past would be forgotten, a mere stack of forged coupons thrown into the stove. All it took was Gabrielle's deserved humiliation.

How did this rivalry begin? They hadn't always been at each other's throats. No, on the contrary, after the first six-day race at the Royal Aquarium in 1895, the two became inseparable. They formed an exceptional connection, the kind that everyone saw but no one ever acknowledged. They were young, they were racers, not normal girls, but *mal-adaptées*.* So long as they continued to race who cared? Others simply called them *les brunettes*. Inwardly, their coach called them *les ténèbres*.†

---

* "misfits"

† "the shadows"

But disapproval, expressed or hidden, would not have mattered. Even with the support of Biblical Law, the judgments of others shrank before Victorine's indifference. Who cared what they thought or even said? It was irrelevant. It belonged on the floor for wiping your feet upon.

That should have meant that Gabrielle bore the burden of navigating social mores for both of them, but no: she didn't care either, but that was because she was in denial.

"It's not love when it's two girls, you shithead," Gabrielle would often say.

That was not really true, of course, but it was forgivable because, at that time, Gabrielle was the only person Victorine did not want to defeat. This rough and sharp being, who was so wonderful and charming in so many ways, to see her was to long to hold her. Gabrielle was afraid. She was afraid of lots of things—of failure, of men, of the upper classes. She was also afraid of the very thing that could have made her fearless. And so, silence became the relationship's sustenance. To speak openly about it would have meant alienating her; to remain silent would allow Victorine to keep her as a friend, the kind she could hold at night after massaging her race-worn thighs.

"Yes, right there. That's the spot," Gabrielle would always say after Victorine had slowly kneaded her way there, starting at her toes.

"Yes, my dear Gabby. I know."

That cold Sunday afternoon in London in 1895, when Victorine walked arm-in-arm with Gabrielle along the Thames embankment and halfway across the Westminster Bridge, she had wanted to own the Thames, pour its tidal potential into her legs, and endow herself with an inhuman might. But harnessing that power was impossible, of course, and what good is a longing if it only works in the imagination? Victorine and Gabrielle formed their unusual and exceptional bond instead. Gabrielle—loud and grumpy, petulant and showy, spiteful, arrogant and prone to wrath, she might have seemed a poor match. But Victorine, despite the limiting epithets of the press, never shied away from conflict, certainly never on the track, but not in her intimate relations either. Besides, Gabrielle's tongue did not cut so deeply once you understood she sharpened it on weakness.

13. Gabrielle Étéogella

The relationship ended abruptly because Victorine didn't return Gabrielle's books. Call it carelessness, but she had been leaving them behind at hotels, in train cars and at train stations and on-board ships. It infuriated Gabrielle.

"By my tally you have to buy me my next ten, you little shit!"

"Don't be absurd, Gabby. You never said you wanted them back. Be reasonable." It was remarkably silly to get so angry over those little booklets which cost only twenty-five *centimes* at the newsstands. "It's not as if you can't afford to replace them."

"That's not the point. They're mine. You return them. That is all. Besides, what am I supposed to read here in England?"

These dime novels, which formed the heart of Gabrielle's diversions between races, were ridiculous. They always depict a young girl, new to the city, arriving from the countryside to work and help her family. But work is a nightmare: either she hides away in some dank garret sewing garments or she withers in the dirty shadows of some factory. Next, she undergoes a series of improbable calamities and winds up without work, home or family. Somehow, despite all her misadventures, she miraculously infiltrates high society: the laundress becomes *La reine de lavoir**; the seamstress becomes *la princesse du rouleau*.†

In gaining access to the upper crust, the heroine learns that the refined, the wealthy and the educated are really monsters. Their affluence, elegance, privilege and knowledge are just masks veiling the horrible truth—their world is nothing more than a brutal, moral hell.

The men were particularly bad. They indulged in all sorts of vices: prostitutes were their society, gambling and alcohol their nourishment and criminal enterprises, like counterfeiting fine art and currency, were their religion.

"I just love seeing how the messieurs lead their lives. Upper class indeed!" seethed Gabrielle. "I'm certain that these stories are all completely true!" Taking a break between heats, she would look up into the stands and find all the beasts sitting up there watching, twirling their mustaches and

---

* *Queen of the Launderette*

† *Princess of the Bolt (of Fabric)*

wiping away at their sweaty brows, *espèces de cochon*!* True, it was only a small handful of men who taunted her and flirted with her, but they were only the boldest. All the others longed to do what these cheeky little brats did openly. Men constituted an entire class of unforgiveable, wanton and despicable predator-tyrant-kings. "Perhaps I was born poor and alone, and they look down on me for it, and think they can exploit my weakness, but they are wrong. I don't need them. I never had that sort of life and I never will. I have known some peace and tranquility, even if I have also known privation and hard work."

In the stories, there was always that one man—the worst in the bunch—who sought to ensnare the young heroine in the web of his evil designs. Part of the pleasure for Gabby was watching the villain fruitlessly pursue the heroine. She always escaped. She was not only resourceful, but principled too, not as little or as helpless as she looked. It gave Gabby great satisfaction.

It was certainly important to keep these men at a safe distance, but working-class men were no better. Passion and error sully the horizons of all families, be they aristocratic, bourgeois, peasant or working-class. No one is immune. Every family is unhappy, and every family protects its shame jealously, imagining it suffers alone, never realizing just how much unhappy families actually resemble each other.

Victorine knew a thing or two about it. Why else race under a pseudonym? It worked better than a shield. Sure, decoding Ollier from Reillo was not a challenge, but Victorine—that was a name that would thwart all detection. And, besides, what better name for a champion? Much better than Éponine. No. Éponine Ollier—it was the name of her father's mistakes. Let him pay for them. His creditors will never find Victorine Reillo! And besides, why not name yourself? When you're left to fend for yourself like that, you've earned that right.

With this name, she could do what she liked, nothing connected her to anyone or anything, no family, no society, no faith, no obligation. Even France was just a place, her language just the tool. She had raced in France, in England, in Belgium, in Germany and now in Russia. And ever since

---

* "pigs"

Gabrielle jumped out of her life, Victorine did not have to acknowledge a connection to anything or to anyone. This did not make her cynical or on the lookout for insults. On the contrary, it allowed her to devote herself completely to racing. If only she were also winning.

As for Gabrielle's stories, rather than blame someone, why not shine a light? Even if it is all true, who wants to be reminded of all that? Rather than look for villains, wouldn't it be much better to have new stories, ones about girls who vanquish their opponents, who heap triumph upon triumph, who earn titles and epithets, not pathetic ones like *Queen of the Launderette*, but titles for heroines so great and powerful they don't even care about aristocrats or anything? The first to summit the gods' mountain because she can eat the entire sky (and she always knew she could too!) She doesn't need to pound her chest against injustice. Revolt, evasion, getaways and close calls don't exist for her, unlike those girls in Gabby's books. No. Above all, the victorious heroine stands with her feet resting firmly on top of her foes—without even noticing. Where is she?

Not in Gabrielle's heart, that's for sure. She saw ugliness and distortion everywhere she looked. More shockingly, Gabrielle sought it out and enjoyed finding it. The stories were just one conduit; nothing could survive her angry glare. *Gabrielle the unlovable and unloving despite being loved.* No, she will never give up her venom. *Pray, God, such anger never seizes me!* That anger taught Gabrielle to read, that anger had taught her to guard her books jealously, that anger prevented her from seeing Victorine clearly, and that anger coloured her perception of all men—including the prince. She had been absolutely rabid about him the entire time of the races:

"That prince—he sure thinks he has some long legs, doesn't he? But he's a small fry. Did you see that Grand Duke last night? Now, that's the radiant blue blood of a true aristocrat! No, ours is just a little prince. Still, watch he doesn't nibble your little ear, Vi-Vi. You might know how to play with wolves, but don't forget this is Russia—even the monks are fat here. Watch yourself, Vi-Vi. The prince has eyes for you."

IV

Prince Dmitri Alexandrovich Shirinskii-Shikhmatov stood alone on the platform of the Tsaroselskii Station to greet his French guests. Out came the young men, one by one, hoisting their bicycles out of the car and rolling them along proudly, pretending they knew where they were going. Imagine the prince's surprise when a team of crinolines and chapeaux filed up behind the men, also bearing bicycles. There were only four of them. Had the men brought their sweethearts?

"These are our *filles-coureuses*,"* explained Lamberjack, a diminutive man with deep-set, narrow eyes and a perfect chevron for a mustache.

"I was expecting French racers, not girls," said the prince in dismay. "No, it will not do, not at all. How can they ride? Will stays† hold up their dresses?"

"We don't wear dresses when we race," scowled Étéogella.

"They are good racers. The competition will be all the richer with them here," offered Lamberjack before Gabrielle crossed a line.

"I don't know about this…" said the prince. "At least there are only four. Let's go. We need to deal with Customs."

The prince's welcome was disappointing, but, no matter, it was still possible to squeeze in training laps while the men were suiting up. Most days, the women trained together. They were eager to maintain their race-readiness and curious to size each other up. There was also the matter of the men: some took the prince's unenthusiastic reception of the women as their cue to keep the track all to themselves. Riding alone was not advisable.

One afternoon, one of the men, Domain, seized his opportunity.

"Enough of that, *midinette!*"‡ he said to Victorine, blocking her path.

Victorine dodged, avoiding a direct hit, but she still bumped him hard enough to knock him over. Victorine lost her balance too, but she got a

---

* "racer" In the early days of cycling in France, racers were called coureurs and coureuses, literally "runners."

† "stays" A synonym for corset.

‡ "dummy"

ot out and dragged it along the track before falling over. The other men shook their heads and laughed heartily.

Furious and red-faced, Domain snapped to his feet, stomped over to Victorine, grabbed her by the elbow and jerked her viciously towards him as he smacked her across the face with his free hand. She recoiled and shouted indignantly.

The prince came out of nowhere. "Monsieur Domain," he began, then said in better French than any of the racers had ever heard before in their entire lives: "We can hardly accept the hitting of ladies at this event. The Mikhailovskii Manège is a respectable establishment. You will need to leave, immediately. I will send assistants to help you pack your things, and I will make all the necessary arrangements for your swift departure." Men in uniform appeared. They seized Domain and escorted him off the track.

"I'm sorry *Monsieur ... P-p-p-rince*. Forgive me. I look at her, with her short hair and her legs, and I... She looks like... It felt like I was just disciplining an insolent boy. All these *coureuses*, I forget they are girls. Please allow me to stay!"

The prince ignored Domain's pleading as the officers unceremoniously rough-handled him. Domain was stupid, yes, but even he knew better than to argue with men in uniform in Russia, especially when a Russian prince was giving the orders. Domain was put on the train that very night and sent back to Paris, alone.

The prince's punishment of Domain was undeniably pleasant to watch, but it also created an awkward mystery. Was it chivalry or justice that had motivated him? Whatever it was, it cast a faint shadow of lukewarm worry over the remainder of her time at the Mikhailovskii. And now what about her crash with Tual, the medical expenses and her extended stay at the Hôtel de l'Hérmitage? How did the prince view his interventions and assistance? Were they all compounding into some type of undesirable repayment? Did he see Reillo *la lionne*? No, he obviously did not. Like all the others, he also saw Reillo *la petite*.

Damn it, he probably saw Reillo *the exquisite* with the *seductive little face* too!

V

"Mlle. Reillo," said the prince as he knocked gently and peered out from behind the broad and elegant door. "How are you feeling today? I hope not too dull. May I come in? I have someone I would like to introduce to you." Behind the prince followed an elderly woman. She was dressed very simply and yet somehow also elegantly.

"This is my old nanny, Sophie. She taught me French and *belles lettres* when I was a boy. I thought she might be able to keep you company during your stay here."

Victorine didn't know what to say. Before her stood a woman who was neither a servant nor a lady. She was not a strong person, but she clearly compensated for that with a certain deliberateness and cleverness in her movements. Had it been necessary for her to do a task, it seemed that she would be able to do it methodically and indefinitely, despite her frailty. The strangest thing about her was that the prince introduced her, this old crow, as his "nanny."

"I'm sure the two of you will get along just fine. Our Sophie is an angel. Soon you will see that, I'm certain," said the prince as he bowed diffidently and excused himself.

The two women looked at each other, each sizing the other up.

After a pause, Sophie heaved a sigh and muttered, "Damned if I know anything about girls who race these newfangled bicycles. What an age we find ourselves in! Who knew it would come to *filles-paysannes de manière garçonnière** staying in St. Petersburg at the expense of the Shirinskii-Shikhmatovs?"

Victorine didn't know what to say.

"Well, you do speak French, don't you?"

Victorine nodded.

"Well, I don't know how I'm supposed to help you. I'm only really good at one thing and that is reading. Do you like stories?"

---

* "peasants tomboys" Simone de Beauvoir uses "filles de manière garçonnière" to describe tomboys in her *Second Sex.*

Victorine was not in the mood at all for more stories, but the drugs were making her a little slow.

"Hmm? Well? You do know what a story is, don't you? 'Once upon a time' and all that? Come on, girl. Did you hit your head? Wake up!"

"Well, since you're offering to read," said Victorine, "what I'd really like is for you to translate the local newspapers for me. I don't read Russian. I should like to know what is being said about m…"

"Don't be ridiculous," snapped Sophie. She muttered something disapprovingly, then asked, "I don't suppose you know anything about Russian literature. Hmm, you probably don't even know anything of French literature… though you must feel something like the Count of Monte-Cristo of late." The old woman nestled into a chair by the window, and from her bag she withdrew a leather-bound and hardcover book, the likes of which Victorine had only ever seen through windows: "No matter. We're in Russia now, so allow me to be the one to introduce you to Pouchkine," and she started reading immediately.

It was irritating to have to let Sophie read. Why the hell couldn't she just read the newspapers? Make no mistake, it was impressive to see how quickly Sophie could translate Russian into French. Really, at times it seemed like she actually was reading in French. If only she would read what one actually wanted to hear.

First, she read Pushkin's fairy tales. These Victorine took in a with polite but strained smiles. Next, she read Pushkin's *Tales of Belkin*. These were better, but why were they always about marriage? Except that one with the undertaker. That was the best story of the bunch.

"Oh, so you like stories about ghosts and crimes—excitement of that sort," said Sophie with open eyes. "Hmm…a little trickster, you are, my mademoiselle. You look so sweet and pretty, but there is much going on inside you, isn't that so?"

Victorine didn't know what to say, so she got back to her original topic.

"Please, I'd much prefer it if you just read me the local papers. I've been in St. Petersburg racing for weeks, and I still don't know what was said about me or the races."

Sophie frowned. "Hmm, I never touch those merchants' rags, but I'll see what I can do."

VI

When Victorine awoke the next morning, the prince was seated across from her bed. It was startling, but it was important not to show any caution or mistrust. Then, she looked past the prince's shoulder to see the doctor, jotting down some notes in a pad.

"What do you say, Mikhail Sergeevich. How is she progressing?"

"The patient is doing well, Dmitri Alexandrovich, but it is crucial that she does not move. We cannot risk infection. And another matter," here the doctor paused and muttered something in Russian, but the word *morphia* could be heard distinctly: "For this reason, I would like to summon a nurse to stay with the girl, to administer."

"Really? Is that necessary?"

"Absolutely."

"What about Sophie? I have Sophie. She will be here shortly. She could take care of it."

"She will have to remain with the girl for the remainder of her convalescence. You must guarantee it, or else I will drop your case."

"I give you my word. I will make all the arrangements."

"Are you sure it wouldn't be more prudent to hire a nurse?"

"I have it under control."

Thus assured, the doctor bade the prince farewell.

"Hmm, well, that's unfortunate," said the prince. "Sophie is going to be irritated. Speaking of Sophie, she told me she has been boring you with Pushkin, or 'Pouchkine,' as she would say. He is a national treasure, of course, but perhaps not the best choice given the circumstances.

"In any case, she mentioned that you wanted to learn what the St. Petersburg newspapers have been saying about the races." The prince walked over to a stack of newspapers and magazines on the table under the mirror. He picked them up and held them out for Victorine to see, raising his eyebrows and smiling. "Naturally, as the race organizer, I have followed the news very closely, and I have kept everything from the last two months. I hope I have exceeded expectations."

The Cyrillic text danced incomprehensibly on the pages, not letters, but the scattered fragments of insects. No matter: the prince will deal with it.

"*Merci, Mon Prince.* Frankly, I no longer had any expectations. This is very welcome news."

"Wonderful! I think it is safe to assume, then, that we share a common interest in this matter," he said smiling through his tidy and dry mustache, resting atop a row of perfect, white teeth.

Victorine nodded, trying not to wince. The pain was awful, but more manageable now that the right kind of stories were on offer. She would have loved another dose of morphia, though, after the doctor's comments, it was now too awkward to bring it up.

"Alrighty! Let's begin, shall we? There is a lot of material!"

"*Merci, Mon Prince.*"

No matter how satisfying it was to have brought the information Mlle. Reillo requested, it was impossible to translate everything. To do so would surely have caused upset. This became apparent when she jumped straight to the most crucial point:

"What did the papers say about my crash?"

The prince vacillated: "This paper says... 'Reillo's crash was terribly unfair,' it says. 'Who was this u-u-upstart Marie Tual, lazily waiting all month long to let the other women take all the prizes only to suddenly d-d-decide to sprint in the last dozen arshins...' erm I should say metres?* 'M-m-madness! Idiocy!'"

That was a very pale account of what had actually happened. No, in reality it was quite different. When the blood spilled out onto the track, the audience became silent. But when her trainer touched the torn flesh on her abdomen, and she cried out in agony, several men started yelling indignantly. Even the prince remembered it, the exclamations of *bezobrazie* and *pozor*† at the sight of such a severely injured girl. Even Gabrielle stopped,

---

* Russia did not adopt the metric system until the Soviet era and it never used the imperial system: one arshin equals 0.71 metres or 0.77 yards.

† Russian: "disgraceful" and "shame"

aghast and gaping. She almost climbed off her Gladiator to help. Surely the press had a lot more to say than "madness" and "idiocy."

It did, but there was no way he could read it to her:

> The races at the Mikhailovskii Manège, as exciting, dynamic and progressive as they had been, nevertheless left the audience feeling bewildered and sad. The races have been taking place every weekend since the New Year, but not a single event has gone by without at least one racer crashing on the high-banked and 'head-spinning' turns and seriously injuring an arm or a leg or both. The last day was the hardest to watch because not only did the men tumble and crash, but the women did too. In fact, the worst crash involved the women. Tual, who had lazily sat back and let the other women take all the prizes all month long, contrary to all reasonable expectation, suddenly decided to compete at full tilt. It was the first time she had attempted to sprint on the track during the entire racing meet, so she had a poor sense of how difficult the first turn was. She entered it too fast, crumpled under her own momentum, and took Reillo down with her.

> Reillo, who had been losing repeatedly to Étéogella, must have been severely disappointed. It was her last chance, and she was positioned to win in this final sprint, only to get taken down by the non-contender Tual. Really, it was needless. Our Russian audience left the races feeling sick and ashamed.

"Perhaps it would be better to read about the January races before your arrival," said the prince as he folded the true account of the crash and tossed it on the windowsill.

That was not an obvious choice, and it would mean that he would not be reading about her February races for a while, but anything was better than those stories Sophie had read to her. And hopefully the prince would withhold less information if he read about the men instead.

So, the prince began:

> Prince Shirinskii-Shikhmatov and Colonel Gelmersen, directors of the St. Petersburg Society of Bicycle Riding have transformed the Mikhailovskii Manège into an international cycling club. Riders arrived from all nations— Germans, Englishmen, Belgians, Americans, and, of course, the French. The Russians arrived in St. Petersburg, too, with representatives from clubs across the Empire, Moscow, Odessa, Vyborg, and some locals from Strelna, Tsarskoe Selo and St. Petersburg.
>
> The manège is unrecognizable. Its normally spartan interior, meant for military dressage, now looks like a fancy horse-racing establishment. It is as if they brought the summer steeplechases at Krasnoe Selo indoors for the winter. No wonder so many members of *le grand monde* are assembled there every evening.
>
> The newly installed electricity makes the manège look even more than miraculous. The entire interior is flooded with electric light. It's literally like daytime inside. The grand stands and loggias sparkle and twinkle, and the new track beams like a virgin beach. The two military bands dazzle with brassy tunes as they thunder out endless joyful marches. Red banners blind you as they gleam majestically between the floor and the rafters. They bear the coats of arms and insignias of all the local clubs, advertising the enthusiasm of the St. Petersburg cycling community, as they shimmer and glisten in the electric glow.

Victorine recalled, when she and her compatriots arrived, they took in the sight of all the regalia and chuckled. No, these Russians will not be able to defeat us. Insignias and coats of arms? That's how the old-timers rode. No, these Russians can buy our technology, but they can't match our mentality. They might as well be racing on *grands-bis*.* Just give me your rubles now and let's be done with it.

Meeting the Russian men only confirmed their suspicions. This is not really going to be a race, is it? Are we going to be competing against ancient family lines, or something? These are not athletes, but bluebloods! How can I race them? Am I really going to be allowed to elbow a prince or a count? In France the wealthy have the decency to sponsor strong blue-collar contenders: 'Let the roughnecks do the racing while we sit back and gamble idly from the stands.' But, apparently, in Russia, the aristocracy and bourgeoisie want to get their hands dirty. Fine, but I will not be held accountable if a duke breaks his neck.

The prince read on.

The crowds were astounding. They demonstrated the intense enthusi-asm of Petersburgers for cycling, not to mention all the out-of-towners who had descended on the "Northern Palmyra" for all of January and February. Tickets were not cheap, and yet there was always a lineup as early as six. They let the spectators in by seven, and, before you knew it, the building was overflowing. How the crowds flooded into the hallways and passages and trickled into every little nook and cranny. Even the first-class loggias were all sold out, and that was where the real money was to be made.

The crowd had a "democratic composition." It would have been pos-sible to have formed a genuine Russian parliament. Everyone was there. The merchants came. Yes, they hid their long beards between their lapels, hoping no one would mistake them for simple hucksters. The clerks came too. They hid their white collars under their scarves, waiting to sneak into more respectable seating when no one was looking. Members of the mili-tary and the bureaucracy attended, many of them known personally to the prince. There were even some grand dames accompanying their grandee husbands. They sat in their fine raiment in the loggias.

---

* "penny-farthing bicycle"

Not everything about the Mikhailovskii Manège was a source of pride, however. Sadly, the track—such a fundamental component—had turned out horribly. Right from the first day, everyone zeroed in on it:

> The track, with its extremely high-banked turns, has been the source of much lively discussion among the men. There is one turn in particular. It was made poorly. Falls are likely to happen, and often too. No amount of training can prepare you for a turn like that. In fact, there have already been some falls during training. Nothing too serious, but serious enough to make it into the French press.

Yes, there had been a lot of complaints about that turn. In fact, Victorine had lost control and tumbled the first time she rode on it too. No wonder it took her down and threw her into this bed. It was a nightmare. When the normally fearless Lamberjack inspected it, he immediately thought whoever first masters it will surely grace the cover of *The Origin of Species*. The other men called it a "sausage maker" and wondered what those damned Russian carpenters must have been thinking when they constructed it. But no matter how much the designer scolded the carpenters (in fact, Finns), they just couldn't understand what they were building. They had only just arrived from Keksgolm, and the last thing they built there was a set of new pews for the Lutheran Church. They were thoroughly mystified by the track, and they firmly believed that by making it more dangerous they must also have been making it better.

When the error in construction was brought to the prince's attention, he made a sour face. It was just that one turn: it curved too abruptly and rose too sharply, making it more like an embankment. He turned to Colonel Gelmersen who simply made a resigned face and said:

"*Tant pis*,* Dmitri Alexandrovich. We start tomorrow. What is to be done? We do what we can, even if we cannot do what we want…"

The races themselves were successful, and they generated a lot of interest. At the opening of each evening, the men would ride around the track

---

* "too bad," or "so much the worse"

in a joyful cavalcade to drum up the interest of the audience. Two bands accompanied this parade from the stands until the loud juror's horn summoned the men to the start. Then, short sprinting events would take up the remainder of each evening, one verst,* one-and-a-half versts, two versts. These were choppy and dangerous. The men raced at breakneck speed. The crowd loved it.

But very early on, it became clear that there was going to be a problem: the French just kept on winning. They outnumbered all the other nationalities, and they dominated every event. Their names almost always occupied the top three positions, and they got almost every kopeck of the prize money.

That's why it was confusing when the prince agreed to spontaneously introduce a hundred-verst race into the program. Sure, no problem. Sometimes they do six-day races; a hundred versts are nothing. If your Frenchmen can do it, I'm sure the Russians can too. So, it was Fischer from Munich; Boulier, Dernocourt, Ducomp and Fournier from France; Luijten from Belgium; and Diakov and Dokuchaev from Russia.

As the prince read on about the hundred-verst race, he again stumbled over his words. He was editing on the fly again. It was embarrassing to reveal the Russians' *naïveté*: "What an opportunity it was to see a long-distance race on an indoor track in January!" "What a marvel this electrification is!" "This never happens in Russia!" "What a lot of cycling enthusiasts we have! They all have stormed Petersburg to see the men race for one-hundred versts." These high spirits revealed an astonishing lack of sophistication. Surely the French never indulged in such exclamations. Why are Russian journalists and the Russian public so simple?

Nothing could have made this clearer than how quickly the enthusiasm descended into boredom. How wildly they applauded for nine laps only to grow silent and even sullen already by lap twelve. "One-hundred versts is more than six hundred laps. At this rate, it will take the men more than three hours to finish," remarked one person. "You really have to love cycling to enjoy this!" exclaimed another. "Aren't they doing themselves harm?"

---

* Versts were another measurement in pre-revolutionary Russia: one verst = 1.06 km or 0.66 miles.

Really, if they had just done some basic maths, they could have figured all this out beforehand. Why did the press think this was newsworthy?

The boredom was beginning its crescendo to impatience when suddenly there was a loud bang. It sounded like rifle fire. Everyone laughed heartily when they realized it was just Diakov blowing a tire. After that, everyone lost interest and went home early. What was the point? The Russians were performing pathetically against the French. Even the journalists left early and collected the results the next morning.

But the audience grumbled when it learned there had been another French sweep: Fournier won 300 rubles, Ducomp won 125 rubles and Boulier won 60 rubles. It was intolerable. The French just kept winning all the prizes. It got so bad that the public started to boo and hiss at the French whenever they entered the track. The cavalcade of racers, once the cheerful opening to every evening, had now turned into a pretext for jealous jeering. Ducomp in particular got a lot of negative attention. Someone actually called him a Robespierre. Exasperated, he threw up his arms, "What do you expect me to do?" he seemed to say.

The prince also glossed over the Luijten-Fischer six-hour race. Who cared about a Belgian racing a German? Frankly, the whole thing wasn't even supposed to happen and came together without any sort of plan just because Colonel Gelmersen had pooled the wagers of an anonymous group of debauched aristocratic youths and then waved a thousand rubles in front of the racers' faces. Honestly, what a waste of time it was! Not a single spectator came out, since the Russian public had made their distaste for long-distance events so clear the night before. Really, the entire thing was hardly worth mentioning, were it not for the interesting detail that neither Luijten nor Fischer succeeded in breaking the record Dokuchaev set in 1896. That year, the Russian rode 196 versts and 125 sazhens* in six hours. Fischer had only managed 187 versts, 327 sazhens and Luijten 186 versts, 203 sazhens.

"And so," concluded the prince triumphantly, "Russia retained its victory even though it did not have a participant in the event this year."

---

* One sazhen = 2.13 metres or 2.33 yards.

But it didn't make any sense for the prince to dismiss the Fischer-Luijten race only to use it as an excuse to rattle his patriotic sabre. It may not have attracted an audience, but it certainly did arouse the interest and support of almost all the racers, at least according to Lamberjack. It began at eleven-thirty that morning. The racers, the judges and a group of leaders gathered in the otherwise completely empty manège.* At first, it was just a hodgepodge of amateur enthusiasts from the St. Petersburg Society of Bicycle Riding. They took turns, either on tandems or on singles, pulling Luijten and Fischer. Quite quickly, however, the racers grew impatient with these amateurs, and the professional racers had to be summoned. Almost all of them came out, eager to support, and the pace livened up dramatically as a result. Lamberjack had recounted how, without the audience or the bands, the entire day was a lively boil of youthful yelling, cheering and laughter. Electricity was not necessary until the final hours of the race: all the men agreed that riding in the daylight was a refreshing change.

Before the race, the competitors had arranged to have a lunch break halfway through. The leaders joined the racers, and all the men ate a glorious meal supplied by Yeliseev's at Gelmersen's expense. They had quite an appetite and devoured fried chicken and drank bouillon. Next, they refreshed themselves with grapes and pears and lemonade (spruced up with a spot of chartreuse). Really, it made one jealous to have missed such a feast.

After no more than eighteen minutes, the men threw aside their meals and refreshments and got on their bicycles again and the race ended exactly as the prince had recounted, only he had neglected to point out that the reason why Fischer and Luijten's distance in six hours was so much less than Diakov's was because they had not benefitted from strong leaders at the start. It was impossible to beat Diakov's record. But that was not really very important. For days after, the men all recalled the event with fondness. Even Luijten had to agree that the day had been memorable for reasons other than the loss of a thousand rubles.

---

* The leaders' job is to ride in front of the competitors and thereby shield them from the air resistance and help them maintain a higher top speed. Leaders rotate regularly so that competitors always have fresh ones.

After the Luijten-Fischer race, the French onslaught continued. They just kept beating the Russians; some whispered it was like Napoleon all over again, only the return to Paris would be a lot more comfortable on the train. Heat after heat after heat they won, so that by the end of each evening thousands of rubles were awarded to them. Colonel Gelmersen quipped that it would be necessary to stop the races in order to save the Russian Empire.

But it seemed that as the crowd got more and more fed up with the French victories, the notoriety and attractiveness of the prizes increased. Even royalty got involved with the announcement of *The Prize of The Most August Representative of the Society of Bicycling Riding, His Imperial Highness, the Grand Prince Sergei Mikhailovich, giving the title of Premier Rider of the North of 1897 and "Champion" of the Mikhailovskii Manège – Twenty-Five Versts*. The First prize was a gift valued at four hundred rubles and a gold medal worth one hundred rubles. Would the Grand Prince really allow a Frenchman to claim this prize? Would the Russians allow such a thing to happen?

Of course not! Dokuchaev took the prize easily. It would have been inconceivable to ask the Grand Prince to hand over such an honour to a Frenchman. But, of course, Victorine had additional insight into this event: Lamberjack, Ducomp, Fournier and Boulier all agreed to restrain themselves so the Russians could win and save a little face. Naturally, she kept this information to herself.

There were great exhibitions arranged for each evening's intermission. These offered an astonishing display of innovation, athleticism and progress. First, some Americans came out to demonstrate a two-wheeled bicycle capable of carrying six people. They called it a sextuplet. It was a wonder to see only two wheels support so many people. What will they think of next? Then, there was the dramatic shot-put competition held in the centre of the track. Again and again, the German men thrust and launched stones from their Adam's apples into the sandy centre of the manège. These Goliaths almost looked elastic as they jerked their entire body into a single effort of defiance. Finally, there was the two-verst stilt-walking race between Moskvitch and Bernault, by far the most popular exhibition. At first, it was the Frenchman in the lead, but by the final laps, Moskvitch took off at something almost resembling an ambling pace, and then he strode past his rival, taking the win with ease. The crowd was very pleased and gave both men standing ovations. After all, it was no small feat, walking on stilts for so long: Moskvitch completed the two versts in 14 minutes, 45 ⅖ seconds and Bernault in 15 minutes, 23 ⅘ seconds.

It was very curious to hear the prince make such a great deal about these intermission exhibitions. That was not how Victorine remembered them at all. The sextuplet was weird. How it navigated the dangerous turn without harming anyone was far more interesting than the vast vehicle itself. Shotput? Dreadful! It was actually difficult to believe the prince was being earnest: how could anyone take any excitement from it when compared to the wheeled sprints? There simply is not any drama in the throwing of stones into sand. And as for the stilt walkers, they plodded along like two giant and elderly birds. How could people applaud them? Fourteen minutes to complete two versts! It is impossible to call it racing. The *piste**
should never have to endure such an insult.

VII

It was at this moment that Sophie appeared at the door.

"Sophie! Come in! We've been expecting you."

Victorine was not happy to see her other reader returned. Sophie was bearing that giant book bag again. More fairy tales? More weddings?

"I am so sorry for my delay Dmitri Alexandrovich. I have had a most unexpected encounter. Just as I was crossing the Anchikov Bridge, I bumped into Lev Nikolaevich."

"Tolstoy?"

"Absolutely."

"What? Well, that is unexpected indeed! I wonder, what is he doing in St. Petersburg?"

---

* "track" or "velodrome"

Tolstoy rarely came to the capital. His visit hinted at something of great importance, but, naturally, it was impossible to know the truth, and it was completely out of the question to ask anything about it. As it turned out, he was here to visit Pavel Biriukov and Vladimir Chertkov before their exile abroad. Tsar Nicholas II was displeased with their involvement with Doukhobors, an agrarian religious sect which sought to bring Eden to earth with protests in the nude and collective non-resistance to violence: this latter point made them conscientious objectors to compulsory military duty and therefore put them at odds with the state. Tolstoy, Biriukov and Chertkov had taken up the Doukhobors' cause against the government, and now the tsar was punishing the two lesser-known men. His Royal Highness would have loved to punish Tolstoy too, but his celebrity was far too great. Of course, no one outside the author's inner circle had any inkling that any of this was taking place.

Sophie considered Tolstoy's presence to be a great and unexpected opportunity. She had always wanted to ask him why he had been so unfair to his humble and self-sacrificing female characters, like Sonia in *War and Peace* and Varenka in *Anna Karenina*. Why so much praise for that spoiled brat, Natasha? And as for that Anna… well, one can only pass over her in silence, really. Needless to say, it was impossible to ask such questions on the street corner, and so she just smiled gently and listened on as a middle-aged man pounded the great author with question after question about his stay in the capital.

"Well, yes. Good for Lev Nikolaevich," continued the prince. "I wonder what he could be up to? Well, let's see now. Where was I? Oh, that's right, stilt walkers and such. Yes, enough of that. Not your cup of tea. I get it."

Here he flipped through another day's paper: "You know, you might enjoy it if I read a little about Murman. He is rather unforgettable."

"I beg your pardon, *Mon Prince*, who is Murman?" Victorine had no recollection of that name.

"You will probably remember him as Zvezdochkin. He is an odd *type*, an *excentrique*, what they call in Russian a *chudak*. Honestly, I've never encountered anyone like him before. I wonder if you get such *excentriques* back in France." There was nothing unusual about adopting a racing name, but Zvezdochkin's approach was unorthodox all the same. On the track, you called him Zvezdochkin, but the second he stepped off the track, you had to call him Murman—or else.

"The name matter derives from some sort of superstition, I suppose. Whatever the reason, he is adamant about enforcing it. My word, he nearly challenged Colonel Gelmersen to a duel, as if it were the old days. The colonel, who lives only to mock his subordinates, called him 'zvezdochka' or 'little star.' My goodness, that really ignited Murman's temper. What a hot head he had! But it was impossible to take him seriously. I think the colonel did not fall far from the mark when he privately labeled Murman 'the clown with the heart of a lion'... or was it 'the lion with the heart of a clown'?"

Oh, yes, it was hard to forget this odd man, this Murman/Zvezdochkin, tall and muscular with an obnoxious crew cut and venomous mustache, decked out in a gaudy, red tricot and short, tight knickers. Now it was clear why his costume had little white stars stitched all over. Yes, this Zvezdochkin—the man of little stars—had distinguished himself in many ways over the course of the tournament. In addition to his peculiar naming ritual and showy outfit, he was the only fellow who did not help out on the pulls during the Luijten-Fischer race. There was definitely something off about him. Lamberjack said of him that, looking into his eyes, one thinks of an inbred hawk squawking angrily at its own shadow.

Surprisingly, on top of all this, Murman/Zvezdochkin was also a rather talented pianist, and he had the irritating need to demonstrate this ability: he would sit at the piano in the tavern of the Hôtel de l'Hérmitage, open the doors wide so all could hear, and then play Liszt's *Hungarian Rhapsody*. He did this every single morning, sometimes playing it through twice before packing it in. "Impressive, but can't he play something else?" "I swear, if I hear that one more time..." "What a blowhard!" the men would say.

As strange as all these things were, there was one last thing worth mentioning about this character, specifically with regard to his conduct on the track: no matter how decisively he lost an event, Zvezdochkin still always appeared, somehow, to be the victor. No matter what the outcome, he was the best, the fastest, the strongest. He would not entertain any other ideas

14. Murman/Zvezdochkin

regarding his abilities. You could see it in his face, which was as firm as a set of quadriceps crushing a crank arm. It must have been something he said to himself, or some decision he made privately in an attempt to manage how others perceived him. It was as if he had placed himself atop a secret mountain, and he allowed himself to pretend that he never needed to descend. Needless to say, all the men hated him.

By the final day of racing, everyone was fed up with his ridiculous behaviour and attitudes. The only ones who tolerated him now were Xidias from Odessa and Smits from France: the former was an opportunist who hoped to win when the others crashed; the latter was a halfwit. The three men rallied gently for five laps when Zvezdochkin, thinking of conquest and mayhem, suddenly shot ahead to be the first to enter the sausage-maker. He was going far too fast and crashed instantly. He slid down the crooked curve like a rotten egg sliding down a failed clown's face. Smits tried to avoid the fallen little-star-man by going around him on the inside, forgetting, remarkably, the inevitability of Zvezdochkin's sliding with gravity. He rode straight into him and tumbled on top of him, yelping like an old dog.

Seeing the fallen men, Xidias seized his opportunity. He climbed to the highest point of the turn to get around the crash, but he went too high, struck the barrier and ricocheted down the bank, sliding into Zvezdochkin and Smits. It looked as if he were an iron filing, drawn irrevocably and inexorably to some Franco-Russian magnetic mass. Zvezdochkin and Smits lay stupefied in agony as Xidias got up, dusted himself off, got back on his bike, and slowly pedaled to the finish, wincing and smiling. The crowd was not cheering.

VIII

Sophie tried her best to sit silently through the prince's reading, but every so often it was possible to hear her sniff and huff indignantly.

"Do you wish to make a comment, Sophie?" the prince finally asked.

"Well, Dima, I always knew these *coureurs* of yours were a gruff sort, but this Zvezdochkin, this *homme aux petites* étoiles, I mean, how could you mix with such people? 'Challenge Colonel Gelmersen to a duel…' Not that I have any particular fondness for the colonel, but, really, how outrageous!"

"Yes, but this fellow really is an unusual case, Sophie. No one else took things quite so far as he did…"

"Really? What about the one who hit this girl? Who was he, a gentleman from La Sorbonne?"

"Well, no," chuckled and nodded the prince, "but that fellow was sent home immediately."

"And on the matter of this girl, who permits a young lady to keep company with men who will slap her? And who allows a girl to ride on a track that nearly kills her? No, Dima, exactly what kind of door did you open with these horrible races? I did not raise you for this…"

Prince Shirinskii-Shikhmatov looked at the floor and said nothing.

What could the prince's nanny possibly know about the *piste*? Listening to her read stupid stories was already irritating; hearing her pass judgment was intolerable.

And yet, it was true that Zvezdochkin was hardly a leading light in the cycling world. And let's not even get started about Domain! But goofs like Zvezdochkin and Domain were few. They cannot speak for all *coureurs*, and they certainly have no connection whatsoever to the *coureuses*.

In fact, thinking about those troublemakers now, in the midst of all the other stories from the races—my, how insignificant they seemed. Listening to the prince read through all these articles reinforced ideas that had not ever been expressed before, but which must have always been there. Now she could see them vividly. She could almost touch them. It was like watching the Lumières Brothers' *cinématographe*, something Victorine used to do with Gabby at the Empire Theatre in London. But, unlike those silent movies, these images were not at all surprising or novel. No, they were absolutely familiar and even dear: the races against friends who had travelled from all over to compete; the machines, beacons of the latest technology, with beautiful, shiny finishes and names like Nimrod, La Gauloise, La Française, César, Le Cerf, Le Globe, Omega, Gladiator and Phébus; the camaraderie and the aspiration that always arise during competition; the skills to adapt to the peculiarities of every track and to take wild risks that end either in crashes or in victory; the shifting tides of adulation and vilification from the audience; yes, even the lying, the exaggerating, the chest-pounding, the self-aggrandizement and all the other outrageous idiosyncrasies of every single participant. It all meant something. It demanded absolute commitment, devotion and total belief. It was more important than a roof, more important than family and more important than a country. The *piste* was home. It was more important than gravity; it was more important than love; maybe it was even more important than winning.

Sophie had no right to pronounce judgement because she had no idea. How could she?

But what about the prince? Even though he built the track and organized the races, he didn't have a clue either. To him, it was all about national rivalry, heaping piles of money, abundant crowds, fascinating spectacles and glowing progress. (Apparently, after reading about Zvezdochkin, clownish tomfoolery was important, too.) And if the prince acknowledged masterful skill at all, it was only as a commodity, not as the result of a significant investment of time and effort. Like a baby reaching out for some shiny trinket, he reached out to the races without fully grasping what was in his hand. It should not have come as a surprise, then, to see that he was so enraptured by the money and the success, and, yet, not only was it surprising, it was disappointing, too. All the best things about the velodrome were just means for him to reach other ends.

And he was wrong. The drama was not in the money, not in the crowds and not in the national rivalry. No, it was not even in the winning or the losing, not exactly. The finish line is just an instant, nothing more than a measuring device. It is precise, yes, but it is not the deciding factor. Every race is already decided beforehand, somewhere off the track. The race is just the dramatization. For example, it was no surprise that Fischer won those thousand rubles—once chartreuse was introduced, Luijten would over-indulge and Fischer would restrain himself. Everyone knew that. Even Luijten knew it: the instant he saw them pour that liquor into the lemonade he said good-bye to all that money. It could not have gone any other way. No mystery there. Likewise, it was no surprise that the French dominated all the events. It was not a question of patriotism or some magical Gallic essence. No, we French are not superheroes: we have a strong tradition of coaches, of training regimens, we have countless tracks and clubs and leagues. We bring a second bike to a hundred-kilometre race so that we can quickly trade it when we get a flat. The French are professionals, not dandies dabbling in fashion. If the prince had wanted to ensure more Russian victories, he should not have invited us, simple as that. No, the prince had it all wrong. He was distorting everything. No self-respecting *coureur* or *coureuse* could ever see it the way he does.

It was not that he didn't deserve to be proud. He had every reason to brag. The event seemed to have been a success. But it was also clear that of all the victors of all the races at the Mikhailovskii Manège that winter, he saw himself, the organizer, as the most victorious of all. You could hear it in his voice as he read. The pride tinkled on the tip of his tongue like a little bell. It was somehow reminiscent of Gabby, who was also very proud of herself, but her pride was more honest, almost childlike: she said exactly the same things in public that she said in dreams and in front of the mirror. It was quite different with the prince—murky. Divining the source and aim of his self-praise was tricky.

Was it just desperation? Yes, there was that, and how embarrassing for a prince, but there was more. It reached far deeper, as if, in exchange for a bargain with some kind of devil, the prince had to be praised ceaselessly. The instant he stopped, thereby admitting he could no longer arouse admiration or applause, the devil could come to collect his soul.

Here, Victorine stroked the bandaged stitches on her abdomen. It was probably time for her next dose of morphia. *Reillo la blessée.** She almost said it out loud, and she thought about her rivalry with Gabrielle. It should have been possible to resist their gamble. It was within one's power to say no. Yes, she had gotten rather caught up in that hot and gusty wind. Does that wind ever make it into a mill or a sail? Well, yes, I suppose it does; it grinds flour for the prince's bitter bread, trims the sail of his infernal vessel. And Gabrielle, she has her wind too, a different wind with different bread

---

* "Reillo the wounded"

and sails. *Le Prince cupide* and Étéogella la courroucée.* Victorine sighed. Perhaps it was time to take her sail down and break bread at a new table.

To gamble everything like that and to inflate oneself into a lioness. I don't actually want that. That's not who I am. Why, if I had to give up racing for the rest of my life and crawl back to my stupid father and all the mess he created just to be healthy and to be free of this pain and this morphine and this prince and his nanny, I know I would gladly do it. I'd rather walk behind a plough for the rest of my days than be the queen of this expensive room for another minute, even if it meant never being able to race again.

IX

Translating into French and editing unfavorable information was becoming exhausting. Moreover, it was not the most engrossing journalism. And besides, none of it had anything to do with Reillo or any of the other women. No wonder Mlle. Reillo looked bored. It wasn't as if the Grand Prince would have given her or any of the other girls that prize. What stake did she have in the Fischer-Luijten race? It would be completely understandable if she felt jealous: there never was a thousand-ruble purse for any of the girls' races.

No, it was true that they had excluded the girls. At least that was the case at the beginning, but it certainly was not the case by the end. It was awkward how things had turned out, given his comments upon the women's arrival.

"Here, let's take a break from the races, shall we?" asked the prince. He grabbed the next paper: "You know it's interesting. Your sponsors will be unhappy, but here they called your bicycle '*zimnii*,' and not 'Zimmy.' That's quite something."

"Why?"

"Well, '*zimnii*' means winter. They're saying you ride a winter bicycle."

"Well that's just ridiculous. It's 'Zimmy,' named after Artie Zimmerman."

"Arthur Augustus Zimmerman, to be precise. Oh, yes, I know all that, but apparently the journalists don't. Your trusty Nimrod 'Zimmy,' out

---

* "The grasping Prince," "Étéogella the wrathful"

of Bristol and made to Zimmerman's demanding specifications. What a lovely and classy machine. I don't like the Gladiator. Didn't that pink girl come out on one?"

"Yes, that was Gab... Étéogella. She rides a Gladiator with the Simpson Chain."

"That Simpson Chain. I don't like that, either," said the prince authoritatively. "Mark my words, innovation will not follow its path."

To look for something not related to racing, to keep things stimulating, the prince scanned the next paper: "Here is an interesting little story. It says in England they have developed a fully functional bicycle, made entirely out of paper."

Victorine looked at him blankly but failed to conceal a smirk.

"It's true! It says 'out of a pressed paper mass, all the parts of the bicycle have been manufactured.' Apparently, they've figured out how to step-up production, and they've even found investors. Well that should be exciting, don't you think?"

"You won't ever find me racing on a paper *bécane*,"* she almost said out loud.

Sensing a lull in their discussion, Sophie stepped in: "Given your activity today, I thought I'd bring this along." It was the latest issue of *Paris-Vélo*. The pink newsprint was unmistakable. "It just arrived this morning."

"Well, there you have it. They finally announced it," said the prince, smiling. "They're going to change the title: it will now be called *Journal des Sports*."

Victorine looked confused.

"Yes, they're changing the name of your lovely pink paper to reflect the evolving interests of its readership. *Paris-Vélo* is over. They're branching out and there will be several new sections added. In addition to bicycle racing, they will now also cover automobilism, yachting, rowing, equestrianism, fencing, boxing, hunting and all other sorts of new developments in athleticism. It's high time, I say."

"But what about *cyclisme*?"

---

* French slang for bicycle, "bike"

"Well, I'm counting on bicycles to continue to grow, but they're going to go in very different directions, and who knows where it will all end up. Take this, for instance. In *Le cycliste russe* they're writing about the electric tandem made by Pinot."

"I think perhaps you mean Pingault, *Mon Prince*."

"If you say so. In Cyrillic it's written P-I-N-O. At any rate, it seems like quite an invention."

"I've seen Pingault's tandem. They raced it at the *piste de Buffalo* in Paris. But that was a joke. It could barely go thirty-three kilometres an hour, it was heavy as lead, and it could only be used for about twenty minutes before the battery gave out."

"Well, that must have been quite a while ago because, according to this, it is now exceeding fifty-four kilometres an hour, and the battery lasts roughly an hour. They figure if they use two tandems consecutively, they can lead a cyclist for more than a hundred kilometres in under two hours. The electric bicycle! Now that's something that could really change the way we do things."

The prince's enthusiasm was understandable, if misguided. The electric tandem of Pingault had in fact once seemed very appealing indeed. To have ridden it with Gabby sitting in the stoker's saddle, to have the advantage of electricity, secretly, while everyone else is forced to use mere muscle power, and to have defeated everyone, almost effortlessly, but, somehow, to have done so no less joyfully. Yes, that had once been a very real temptation. Four legs cranking, united by an electrical drive train. It would have been almost as good as riding with the Thames estuary in her legs. The fantasy of holding such power had once appeared as attractive as honey; now it just looked impossible.

X

No, it was more than boredom. Something definitely had changed in Victorine. She was always rather laconic, so it was difficult to know, but perhaps it had been too long in postponing the reports about the women's races. It was awkward. He had never explained to Victorine or the others why he had suddenly changed his mind about allowing them to race. Truth was, he had to: by the fourth weekend of racing, crowds had already started to dwindle. The club members were starting to complain. Something had to be done.

"We should have foreseen the boredom," said Colonel Gelmersen, one hand on each cheek. "Round and round they go. At least roulette offers the chance to win; this is mindless. Sure, the names change, but otherwise it's just the same thing every evening. What were we thinking? At least we still have the military aspect to look forward to…"

"But we're still waiting on the Styrias. Iokhim's has not followed through on its commitment." The prince and the colonel were waiting on some folding bikes to arrive from Austria in order to give a demonstration of the bicycle's military potential. The plan was to have soldiers ride the Styrias on the track. But these folding bicycles were a new design. Not a single model had been built when the prince and the colonel put in the order.

Without the Styrias for the soldiers, they needed a fix. Those troops were just sitting around, waiting in the wings. It could only lead to trouble.

"What about the girls?" suggested Gelmersen.

"What of them? You don't mean to suggest that we actually let them ride?"

"Dmitri Alexandrovich, what choice do we have?"

"But there are only four. Won't the public get even more bored?"

"*Tant pis,* Dmitri Alexandrovich! We'll have to make do."

"And they're all French. We lack the element of nationalistic rivalry. What do they offer to satisfy the crowds?"

"Give them a try! What harm could they possibly do? And if things go poorly, what is to be done? You don't restrain yourself when the bottle is first opened, nor do you hold back when you've made it to the dregs!"

In the improvised changing area behind the manège, the four women sat idly over dinner in conversation. Lamberjack had brought them some smoked salmon, salted salmon caviar, little dumplings called *pelmeni*, pickled mushrooms and a couple of bottles of Borjomi mineral water. The women thanked the kind Lamberjack and then told him to scram, which he did with his usual warm smile. They sat in a circle relishing the meal.

"The calendar says it's the ninth of February, I think," offered Marie Tual.

"Yes, but what about for us, for normal, French-speaking girls, please?" asked Victorine.

Just then the servant entered and invited the women to the track. It was time to race.

"You heard him," said Gabrielle without missing a beat. "To hell with the date, you numbskulls. Get your shit together and let's go!"

Gabrielle stuffed her face before tearing into her duffle bag to get her outfit. She looked at the others' dull black jerseys and tricots and threw on her pink outfit, the one with the ribbons attached at the shoulders from which two white streamers streamed and flowed as she rode. She tied another white ribbon around her waist. And then she undid her long, wavy hair. It nestled over her shoulders. It would flow and billow quite nicely as she rode. Russia had never seen the likes of her before—that was certain.

The women were permitted to ride a few warm-up laps, to get acquainted with the crowd. It was their version of an opening cavalcade, which had always been extended to the men. Of course, the men had a much larger parade, but, perhaps, these girls might make a similar impression.

At first, there was absolute silence in the manège. A few voices offered their support and hands clapped, then, rapidly, the entire crowd started roaring with enthusiastic applause. They were especially pleased to see Étéogella in pink and with her long hair. Many commented on how attractive she looked. But they remarked on the others, too—their svelte figures and those tidy and trim black outfits.

The crowd's voices awakened the women's muscles and aroused their need for victory and for domination. It flowed through their veins and ignited their hearts.

As they rode around the track, Reillo and Étéogella started testing each other out. No one else understood or appreciated, but these were much more than tests of strength and ability. Would it be reasonable to expect kindness? A smile? No, it would not.

The first event was the one-verst sprint, six laps at top speed. Right from the start, Étéogella tore away from the group with Mlle. Reillo right behind her. Mlles. Georgette and Tual competed for last place. There was no way Gabby could maintain that pace, and, by lap three, Victorine tore ahead. But then there was that damned, mad curve: she always had to slow down to get through it; meanwhile Gabby, who had mastered it by lap five, took it at top speed and sped past Victorine before the finish. Victorine was only a half-wheel behind.

Next, the prince read about the one-and-a-half-verst race. Étéogella won that one too, but not without having a fight with Reillo. It was still shocking to think about it, Étéogella's pink elbow landing sharply in Reillo's neck and cheek, forcing the smaller rider to recoil and let out a frown and a yell. It didn't seem fair to let the bigger one hit Reillo. But it was so outlandish to see women hit each other, deliberately and with strong elbows, no less. It felt like another world, one that could not be interfered with. Étéogella took another seventy-five rubles for first. Again, Reillo took thirty-five for second.

As the prince read more and more about the women's heats, it became more and more clear that Mlle. Reillo must have really disliked Mlle. Étéogella. Always losing to the same person, especially frustrating considering how many flying elbows seemed to earn her those wins. Indeed, recollecting that loud, sailor-mouthed Étéogella was becoming irksome. Her pink outfit and ribbons now looked more like mocking gall than comeliness. The prince started to skip ahead, hoping to find a race where Victorine won.

"Let's see," searched the prince. "Here we are! 'The ladies came out again. This time, right from the start, they took off at a brisk gallop,' that's interesting to compare you to horses. 'Étéogella took off energetically in her pink *foofayka*…' erm jersey, I suppose, would be the right word here, 'with a *tricolore* ribbon across her chest. Again, Reillo was her main rival, but Étéogella finished ahead yet again. The distance was one-and-a-half versts, with Étéogella coming in at three minutes and eight seconds, and Reillo just a half wheel behind. Marie Tual came in third with a time of three minutes and $9/15$ of a minute.'

"I think I'll skip ahead again. Let's see… Here, yes, 15 February. I remember that day, we had finally relocated Mlle. Georgette. *Mon Dieu*, she gave us so much trouble, disappearing all the time! I'm scared to ask what she got up to. And your French men had just come back from Moscow. It says here that they experienced a 'fiasco' there. Do you know anything about that?"

Victorine did. Apparently, the men had overdone things with some Muscovite paper men. Too much vodka. They completely lost their minds, and, of course, the Russian calendar completely confused them. There was no hope of returning to Petersburg any earlier than the eleventh hour.

"So, we'll skip over the men's heats and, here we are, 'The cavalcade of ladies appeared just before the second heat. The audience again received the ladies warmly. It was all the same competitors from last week. They wore their tight, black tricots and form-fitting knickerbockers and stockings. They cut flexible and strong figures. Étéogella again wore her pink outfit.

"'The distance was one verst. Tual began with a shot of luck to take the lead early, but at the very end Étéogella caught her. It looked like another win for pink until Reillo snuck up from behind and passed her nimbly and easily. Étéogella swerved sharply to jockey Reillo, but the little lady in black got past and got the win with a time of one minute, fifty-two seconds. This time it was Étéogella who was half a wheel behind.'

"Well, there you are. You won that one, didn't you? You really showed her! Let's see, what else we can find."

He inevitably came to Fokin, the Russian man who raced the French women because he was too clumsy to race with the men. His first crash occurred when he took the difficult turn too fast. He came a cropper, right in front of the judges' table. His next crash took place the following weekend. He was just warming up before the races when he smashed into Alexandrov. It looked as if an occult force yanked Fokin from his saddle and smacked him hard on the track. He suffered a concussion and could not participate in racing at all that evening.

The next day, Sunday, it was decided to allow Fokin to ride again. Let him race with the *damochki*,* if he still wants to race.

---

* Russian: "the little ladies"

"That's just great!" exclaimed Étéogella when she learned about Fokin. "If that nincompoop comes near me, I'll lose my mind. I'm not getting taken down by that maimed piglet."

Victorine couldn't have agreed more, and she resolved to do all she could to keep ahead of him.

Whereas, before, the ladies' competitions were regarded as a form of diversion from the main event, the organizers billed the race against Fokin as a great Russo-French match. National pride was, quite suddenly, at stake. At last, there was a chance for the Russians to show these Frenchies how to race.

Fokin pulled up to the start with bandages around his head and on his hands. Meanwhile, the "damochki" looked fresh and ready for any sort of action. They did not even show the slightest trace of exhaustion despite the days of heavy racing already behind them. Étéogella showed up in pink again. Her frizzy plait of dark hair, bound with a pink ribbon, bounced easily between her shoulders.

The race began.

In the time it took the ladies to do two laps, Fokin had only done one-and-a-third. He gave up trying after five. Meanwhile, Reillo really took off, dropped everyone, and, with a time of three minutes, fifty-three and ⅘ of a second, won the race.

"It doesn't mean shit because of stumblebum!" said Gabrielle as she rode up alongside Victorine.

"What do you mean? I won it. It counts."

"Wrong again! No one cares *who* wins. Victory goes to the national group. *La France* won, *not you.*"

On the last day of racing, there had been some mixed tandem races. Tual shared with Fokin, Reillo with Ducomp, and Étéogella with Xidias— Murman/Zvezdochkin refused to ride with a woman. It was an interesting exhibition, but not a serious race.

But when the "Foreign *Damskii* Race" started, there was much lively interest. Only two ladies volunteered to participate, Reillo and Étéogella. They made some kind of agreement. It seems like it must have been for a rather large sum. Meanwhile, the audience murmured. Some considered it a dead heat; most put all their faith in Étéogella. Distance—one verst or six laps. Étéogella abandoned pink for this race and wore a black tricot for the first time; her hair was tied back neatly too.

Right from the first lap it was clear that victory would go to Étéogella. She crossed the finish line with a time of one minute, forty-three and ⅘ of a second. Reillo was less than a second behind.

The final race was the women's handicap. It was the race where Tual crashed and took Victorine down with her. The outcome of this race is already known.

The prince finally got to the part when the Styrias arrived from Austria. It was on the penultimate day of racing. The soldiers came out with the bicycles folded up and strapped on their shoulders. They marched across the sandy centre of the manège ceremoniously as the military band accompanied them with a vibrant march. Then, in unison, the soldiers marched up to the starting line, unfolded the Styrias, locked them in their open position, and then waited for the command to mount. Once commanded, they lifted their legs, again in unison, and sat astride their vehicles. As the soldiers rode around the track, it became clear that they could navigate the difficult sausage-maker turn easily: their vehicles were heavy and they rode slowly.

"You'd think that would be it, that there's nothing left," said the prince, "but guess what? There's more!"

There was something unsettling in the prince's tone and face. It felt like he had been planning to finish like this all day long.

"Do you remember that fellow Domain? That ruffian who disrespected you so? It seems that he did not really learn his lesson. Have a listen to this:

> "The French racers might have all returned to Paris for good, but they have shown that their time here has left them full of deep Russophile sentiment. They were extremely upset and offended when they learned how Domain, who had returned earlier than them, could

allowed himself such uncomplimentary remarks about Russian hospitality. "If anyone is guilty of breaking the rules of decorum in Petersburg, it is Domain," said all the Frenchmen. He permitted himself a great excess when he struck his colleague in the face, and in the presence of witnesses too. This insult, so contrary to the spirit of French gallantry, led to Domain's deserved expulsion from Russia."

Victorine met the prince's smile with a cryptic air, looked at her lap and said, "Mme. Sophie, could you please give me a dose of the morphia? I am finding the pain a little unmanageable at the moment."

"Right," stammered the prince. "I guess that means it's time for me to go."

XI

Even though Prince Dmitri Alexandrovich Shirinskii-Shikhmatov found it tiresome to tailor the news stories for Mlle. Reillo's consumption, privately, he really could not read enough about the races. He was so proud of himself. True, they had not exceeded his expectations or hopes, but how could that ever happen? No, concessions had to be made. Such were the times. Boyhood under Alexander II and youth under Alexander III had prepared him poorly for adulthood under the newly crowned Nicholas II. But he was learning about the new world, adjusting to it, and he was adjusting his expectations too. He might not ever be able to return to the family estate, but he had managed to secure a foundation for cycling in St. Petersburg.

The biggest feat by far was getting all those racers from abroad and from all over the empire too. That really sent a message. St. Petersburg can become a racing centre, not as important as Paris, of course, but important all the same.

As for the women, well, that turned out to be a happy accident, though, to be frank, they were no more than a diversion. It was not as if a general interest in women's racing would miraculously emerge. Whenever he flipped through those issues of *The Russian Cyclist* he felt incredulous. Every week they had an illustration of a lady riding a bicycle on the cover, and they had devoted two entire issues to the theme of "The Bicycle as an Instrument of Women's Emancipation." But, on closer inspection, these articles read more like *zhitia** than reality. These were icons, not real women, at least not real Russian women: there was a Mlle. Linon, Mme. Pinot, Mme. Chouet. French names always look so deflated and maimed in the Cyrillic alphabet. No, there was not a single Russian among them, which in any case would have been impossible. Women might make up a large market share in England, France and America, but that could never happen here. The grand dames—countesses, princesses, duchesses—are not going to start riding bicycles and wearing bloomers. And no matter how wealthy they become, it is inconceivable to imagine a merchant's wife in rational dress. This was Russia. Women's cycling will not come here. Karl Marx and the populists will control Russia first. *The Russian Cyclist* is just wasting paper and misleading people. We need not ever think about women racing in the Mikhailovskii Manège ever again. Let's forget about the whole thing.

A second, and perhaps more important, accomplishment was the procurement of those folding Styrias from Austria, and the demonstration of the bicycle's military potential. It was not that there was any special reason to get excited about bicycles in the military, or that they possessed any genuinely valuable contribution to Russia's might on the battlefield. It was only that the presence of cycling soldiers at the Mikhailovskii Manège ensured that various government agencies, both at the municipal and at the imperial level, would be satisfied: Prince Shirinskii-Shikhmatov had met his commitments and undertakings.

In truth, it was Colonel Gelmersen's idea to get the army involved. It was an unorthodox idea, like all his ideas, but it ended up doing the trick. But, goodness, wasn't he a weirdo, a real white crow. He belonged to one of those German families that came here generations ago, during the reign of Peter the Great, to help modernize the army. Their usefulness had

---

*   Russian: "lives of the saints," or "hagiography"

long since become diluted, but their presence persisted. In any case, they weren't going back.

The colonel had useful connections, not only thanks to his notable career in the military, but also, and more importantly, with the Sheremetiev family. This truly was a golden asset. If, as the saying goes, "All roads lead to Rome," then in St. Petersburg it is better to say, "Forget Rome, just find the road that leads to the Sheremetiev's front door!"

Gelmersen had earned the ear of Sheremetiev through his service to the count's private fire brigade, which he named after Peter the Great. A modern city needs a good fire brigade. Indeed, the tsar himself was especially grateful, and he allowed the count and all his captains, including Gelmersen, the special privilege of leaving any royal function at any time, so long as the brigade's fire-fighting services were required.

From Count Sheremetiev's point of view, Gelmersen was a twit and a troublemaker who needed supervision and management, and the only reason for enlisting the colonel's services was to prevent him from destroying the next generation of Sheremetievs with his pernicious influence. The colonel had landed the role as raconteur, cynic and rake, and the younger Sheremetievs loved him for it. They regularly invited him to various functions for their amusement. The young aristocrats would gather around him and chortle whenever he extemporized cynically on any subject. No matter what he was talking about, his story would always end with the exclamation, *tant pis*, often with outcomes that could be, admittedly, quite amusing. It all would have been relatively harmless had he not also earned the reputation for spreading gossip more venomous than accurate, and for generally letting things deliberately and gleefully go to the devil. The count was hardly pleased with these hijinks and resented the colonel for them. It would have been necessary to plunge the old sponger into the Neva with an anchor tied to his feet had it not turned out that he was as competent an organizer in the fire brigade as he was a card sharper. In the belief that responsibility reforms, the count promoted the colonel who, indeed, ceased allowing things to go to the devil, at least whenever a fire was involved. He still sat back and leisurely giggled whenever a young count frittered away his inheritance at cards, but he never once allowed a building to burn to the ground, at least not without a good fight.

As for bicycles, Count Sheremetiev was accustomed to unorthodox requests from Gelmersen, but this one confused him more than
Mendeleev's lectures on the Periodic Table.

"What, pray tell, seized you to throw yourself into bicycles and racing?"
asked Sheremetiev. "Surely, this is just a fool's errand. I mean, honestly!
Bicycles! I fear that you will finally waste yourself on this one, Colonel. I
consider these wheeled vehicles to be another instance of that same deca-
dence which threatens to devour our poor, nascent, merchant class."

"Your excellency, I do understand your concern for our poor merchants,
but I think you are being too zealous. There is much here that is good, not
only from an econ... eco... erm economimo-industrial perspective."

"Econom...im...o...mo?" One thing that really annoyed Sheremetiev
was Gelmersen's peculiar tendency to stack additional syllables on his
words. It was confusing and raised suspicion: was he really such a sim-
pleton, or was this just one more example of the old buzzard's rabid and
scornful cynicism?

"Your Excellency, perhaps you hadn't considered bicycles from the
milititar-cavalaro point of view."

"Militita-tara-what?" Sheremetiev brushed his hands in front of his
face, exasperated. "You're saying there's a military angle to all this?"

"Indeed!"

"Alright, I'm listening."

"Well, just as the steeplechase hardens our officer corps and keeps
its edge sharp in times of peace, so, too, might the bicycle race do the
same thing."

"Redundancy! Why finance bicycles when we already have horses? And
if our gentry must ride the bicycle, then they can pay for it themselves. No,
there is absolutely no need to get the Imperial purse involved."

"But, yes, Your Excellency, of course you're right. But perhaps you
hadn't considered the technocico-strategical superiority of the bicycle on
the battlefield?"

"How's that?"

"Well, Sergei Dmitrievich, a bicycle does not require food or shelter.
A bicycle can be carried easily by one person. A bicycle can transport all
sorts of materiel to the front for combat. A bicycle is an exceptional device

when it comes to conducting espionage. A bicycle can never be startled by artillery fire, or, generally, ever get the heebie-jeebies the way a horse does. And, Sergei Dmitrievich, consider: a bicycle cannot die."

Count Sergei Dmitrievich thought this through. Though his better judgment told him to turn and walk away, especially when Gelmersen said 'heebie-jeebies,' he had to concede that the colonel raised good points. But, damn it, he really hated admitting it.

How he despised those gangly bicycles. State-of-the-art, yes, but to what end? He'd never heard anyone suggest a military angle before. From what the count could discern, all that bicycles had accomplished up to that point was in the name of frivolousness, egotism and vanity.

The first time he ever saw these contraptions was when he visited His Imperial Majesty, the Late Alexander II, at the Winter Palace at Christmas. The tsar's sons had just received some of these wheeled gadgets as gifts. Just imagine, heirs to the throne, prattling on enthusiastically about *vélosipèdes*, explaining that mastering these devices was difficult, a skill best acquired on a flat and even surface. What better surface than the parquet floors of the Winter Palace, especially when it was minus twenty-five degrees outside? How it galled Sheremetiev to see those two boys, one on a quadricycle, storming through the grand halls, bursting past Michelangelo's *Crouching Boy* and actually bumping into Rembrandt's *Prodigal Son*. Catherine would have thrashed those two boys to within an inch of their lives!

But a new century was just around the corner. New military needs were emerging and opportunities did need exploring. If Gelmersen could make something useful out of these *velosipedy*, more power to him. Maybe the old codger-sponge would finally grow up and stop corrupting our young men. If you can pull it off, good for you; if you fail, it's the fire brigade forever. *Et tant pis pour vous!**

"And you intend to use these races to develop the military angle, specifically?"

"Yes, of course, the militataro-cavallero-bicycles. Just as in steeple-chases. Any development must support the militit-operational potential!"

"All right, Colonel Gelmersen, I have my reservations, but let's see what you can do."

---

* "and so much the worse for you!"

"Rest assured, Sergei Dmitrievich, there is still ample gun powder left in my powder keg!"

"Yes… well, be that as it may, I want you to explore the domestic production of some military devices for exposition in your races. Russian manufacturing should be able to form a wedge, leading the world in producing war machines of this sort."

"Most assuredly," falsely assured Gelmersen who had already made inquiries about the Styrias in Austria.

All this talk about the military came as an absolute surprise. Who had ever heard of such a thing? Lying to Count Sheremetiev made the prince feel extremely uneasy. Of course, Gelmersen should take the lead when dealing with the count, but bicycles on the battlefield? It was pure fabrication, wasn't it?

"Fear not," reassured Gelmersen. "I was just, as the saying goes, directing the water into the mill. Either I have the golden hands or I am just a great, big pancake. Whatever turns out to be the case, you have my word that I will work tirelessly. No matter what happens, I promise I will never leave you holding your nose. My word of honour, Prince Dmitri Alexandrovich."

XII

With Count Sheremetiev's endorsement, the prince and the colonel went to see Nikolai Vasilievich Kleigels, the mayor, in order to present their case about bicycles coming to St. Petersburg.

Be they for recreation, competition or warfare, nothing could have been further from Kleigels's mind than bicycles. He had been entrusted with the enormous task of increasing St. Petersburg's electricity supply. The 1868 Co., which had supplied the Winter Palace and its environs with electricity since, well, 1868, was now losing its monopoly. Other administrative districts of the city now sought to expand electrification to their residents and businesses. Offerings were coming from numerous fronts; Helios from Germany had made the most robust offer. In the meantime, numerous independent gasoline and natural gas generators started popping up. It was getting out of hand. The city needed a comprehensive plan that would spread electrification across the entire Petersburg region like honey over toast.

People were getting impatient with the darkness. In America, Edison was not only offering electricity to light up the cities, but also to cook, to heat and to sew. Meanwhile, in the Russian capital they were still bumping into each other on the streets at night, bumping into their walls and doorways and even bumping into their oil lampposts. Sure, Pushkin had lauded how the city was borne from out of the darkness of the forest and the impenetrable swamps, but time was up. The twentieth century was quickly storming in, and something had to be done.

But, for now, the electrical question would need to be solved on a district-to-district basis. For example, Rozhdestvennyi District was being deprived of electricity because the Helios Company could not meet demand. Even though the residents opened their pockets as wide as they could go, Helios only agreed to extend electricity into the Peski Cathedral. Everyone else would have to make do with lamps until Helios found a solution—so what's that? Forty more years of kersosene?

Why on earth had Peter the Great moved the capital to this vast and flat flood plain? It is not even possible to set up a viable sawmill. The closest waterfall was at Imrata along the Vuoksi River. Kleigels had sought development of a hydroelectric dam there and had just learned that morning that the Finns had declined, despite the exceptional generosity (mixed with some Russian strong-arming) that seasoned the offer. But the Finns were intractable. Why are they so cagey? You'd almost think they'd rather flood their own duchy than share any of its wealth. Russian plants would have been of great benefit to them too.

Kleigels would have begged the Finns were it not for the deal's numerous shortcomings, the principal one being the need for heavy French investment. Yes, foreign capital would have been necessary at Imrata, without question, though the contract did stipulate that the city would have the option to purchase the hydroelectric installation from the investors in 1918, at which point the Imperial capital would emerge as an energy independent city. St. Petersburg, a model for the world. Too bad it fell through. No matter. A solution would be found. One way or another, Russia will be a marvel in the twentieth century.

In the meantime, Kleigels was grateful to get a break: enough about electricity for a while. Now to discuss this outlandish, but captivating proposal by Prince Shirinskii-Shikhmatov and Colonel Gelmersen.

"I see," said Kleigels upon hearing the plan. "So, it is your intention to showcase these races from the military point of view. The latest technology and how it enhances the fighting spirit." Kleigels, a former military man himself, could feel the old pulse gathering in his loins. "Yes, quite good. I should say. And have you selected a location?"

"Err, location?" Unforgivably, neither Gelmersen nor the prince had given this any thought. "Well, frankly we had thought of deferring to you and your formidable acquaintance with the facilities of the city."

"Splendid, how about the Mikhailovskii Manège?"

"The manège? Well, yes," chimed in the prince. "I suppose that would be large enough to build a decent track and to hold spectators."

"I should certainly think so! And, yes, its formal connection to the cavalry and to dressage. Yes, quite good! And, to be frank, there is a plan afoot to change the manège into an exhibition building, promoting industrial development and entrepreneurialism and that sort of thing. In other words, your event is perfect. All the pieces will come together into one whole." Kleigels was sitting up straighter in his seat now.

The prince paused before asking his next question: "Mayor Kleigels, Your Excellency, has any electricity been extended to the Mikhailovskii?"

"How's that? Ermm… electricity you say?" This really was like getting snow dumped on your head. Damn it! Do you need to be an electrical engineer to do this job?

"Well, yes, Mayor Kleigels. Of course, we should have electricity," persisted the prince. "I dare say it would greatly improve the general impression. It will be January and February when we hold the races. Kerosene will be fine, I suppose, but it is not exactly, as the English say, 'on the cutting edge.'"

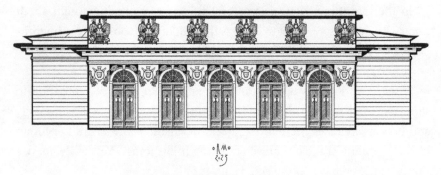

15. The Mikhailovskii Manège

"Too true," conceded Kleigels, crestfallen.

Here, the prince was being disingenuous. It was absolutely essential to have electricity. If it had meant holding the races in the throne room of the Winter Palace, he would have insisted. Nothing less than electrification would do. Otherwise the event would just be a bunch of ruffians chasing each other around a wooden track. In order for this to work, it had to be an impressive spectacle, worthy of the times.

Just then, someone appeared at the door. His attire was stunning, but altogether too dramatic. Clearly a foreigner or an entertainer of some sort, he took one look at the prince and the colonel, bowed dramatically, and apologized with a very heavy accent.

"My word! The time," exclaimed Kleigels, his carp eyes popping out above his frizzy, saggy mustache. "Signore Ciniselli, please come in. I am very sorry, gentlemen, for this conflict of schedules, but, as luck would have it, all of you have come to me with a connected matter, or at least, you are now all connected in one important matter."

Upon seeing the two bluebloods seated in Kleigels's office, it seemed to Signore Ciniselli that he would have to make another appointment. This was very vexatious. He had come to Kleigels in the hope of renegotiating the terms of the electrical supply to his circus on the banks of the Fontanka Canal, just around the corner from the Mikhailovskii Manège. Would his enterprise be better served by Helios? Should he remain with the 1868 Co. or should he buy his own generator?

To help facilitate negotiations, Signore Ciniselli had brought over some fresh cannoli, very hard to come by in St. Petersburg, and a favorite of Kleigels. When Kleigels invited Ciniselli into his office despite the presence of such hifalutin guests, the circus maestro was so relieved that he couldn't restrain himself.

"Your Excellency, I have brought you some fresh cannoli prepared over at Domenico's. I brought them straight here."

"Signore Ciniselli, you know I cannot resist cannoli, but what about my other guests?"

"Your Excellency! You insult me! Of course, I have arrived with a more than generous supply!"

Here, a heartily laughing Kleigels introduced Ciniselli to the prince and the colonel. Ciniselli was more desirous to eat the cannoli than Kleigels, if that can be believed, and he took out four cannoli and requested four plates, forks and napkins.

"Cannoli, you say," offered Colonel Gelmersen skeptically. "I don't think a real man would ever admit to eating such a thing! It sounds like trouble."

"Don't be silly, Colonel! Signore Ciniselli has been bringing me cannoli for quite a while now."

"Fear not, Colonel Gelmersen!" exclaimed Ciniselli. "News of your flirtatious brush with my cannoli will never leave these four walls. Your secret will be safe with me!"

Even the prince smiled at this.

"Now, let's get down to business, shall we?" asked Kleigels, already licking his fingers through his mustache. "As it turns out, both parties are here in the search for a solution to the problem of electricity. Truly, it seems, the question of the ages. Here is what I propose. There is the option of buying a generator. You can plunk it down in the Fontanka in a moored vessel. It need not take any space on the street. It will be fueled by petrol. They did precisely this over at the Malyi Theatre, also on the Fontanka. You will need to petition Active Privy Councillor Goremykin in Internal Affairs. Not only is he the one to petition for licensing for an industrial exposition, such as yours, Prince and Colonel, but he will also be able to secure the licensing for the generator, which, I declare, you will need to purchase, Signore Ciniselli. Prince Shirinskii-Shikhmatov and

Colonel Gelmersen will pay you some sort of fee, I suppose. They will only require it intermittently for about eight to ten weeks, though there are other functions being held at the Mikhailovskii; perhaps you can make a more permanent arrangement with the administration there. I leave all the particulars for you to sort out amongst yourselves."

Kleigels took a deep breath, stuffed the rest of his cannoli into his mouth, wiped his beard with a kerchief and smiled:

"Right, so have I satisfied everyone's queries? I think, in your case, Dmitri Alexandrovich and Colonel Gelmersen, it would be advisable to take your request up a few strata. So, I received Count Sheremetiev's petition on your behalf, very good. Did the count, by any chance prepare other petitions?"

"Yes, in fact. He has already connected this matter to His Most High Excellency Goremykin."

"Splendid! I will add my name in support. I'm certain that everything will flow as if it slid atop warmed butter."

Warm butter indeed! Entrusting the event's electrical supply to an Italian ringmaster was a little bit too progressive for the prince.

"What are you worried about, Dmitri Alexandrovich?" countered the colonel, chuckling with a hint of exasperation. "Do you suppose the Italians will send over one of their clowns to disconnect us? Don't be so uptight. Standing alone on the battlefield does not make one a soldier."

XIV

Even with the support of Count Sheremetiev and Mayor Kleigels, to address Active Privy Council Goremykin directly about bicycles would have been unwise. Thankfully, Dmitri Alexandrovich's older brother Andrei was a member of Goremykin's staff.

"Really, Dima, is this the wisest use of your time and resources? Why not let me ask around, and I'll try to get you a position here at Internal Affairs? I do not think it is proper for men of our station to be soliciting the Ministry of Internal Affairs in the name of bicycle races. The Empire needs our efforts elsewhere. We have a duty."

16. A Clown from the Ciniselli Circus

Easy to say when father practically threw you into the civil service. No, the bureaucracy was no place for Dmitri. True, his brother did well and he had security. But to be an entrepreneur, a purveyor of bicycles, this was all new, and no one had any idea where the ceiling might be.

"We just need a license, Andriusha. We wish to hold a race to promote the bicycle in the Empire. We also intend to open a bicycle shop in order to sell bicycles in the aftermath of the races. We considered it prudent to consult with you, first, but if you won't help us, we will use the official channels."

Gelmersen wanted to kick the prince, hard, under the table: "Andrei Alexandrovich, all your brother's talk about business does not connect to the main thrust of our enterprise, which includes, or, I should say showcases, the importance of the bicycle from the soldier's perspective..."

Andrei smirked at Gelmersen and just shook his head. He turned to his brother and said: "And what is this you say about setting up shop, do you mean to sell these vehicles in St. Petersburg?"

"Yes, we found an excellent location on Canal Griboedov, across from Kazan Cathedral."

"Your proposed location is uncomfortably close to the site of His Imperial Majesty's assassination? ... Hmm? ... Ah, well, my friends! It seems the time for our consultation has ended. I must get back to work on my report. The peasants of Poland will not be kept waiting a moment longer."

Despite any reservations at the Ministry of Internal Affairs, official support was granted, the licenses and documents materialized, arrangements were made with the Mikhailovskii, and the contract formalized and signed with Signore Ciniselli. Foreign racing organizations, Styria in Austria, hotel reservations, entry and exit visas—the entire organizational headache was taken care of. The bicycle, its proponents, its entire value system would carry the prince into the twentieth century after all.

XV

Since the prince's departure, a few things became very clear: first, Victorine got her period, and, consequently, she had a much better sense of the date; second, she re-evaluated her position on what might be a more suitable name for her in the press. True, it was wrong to call her "*la petite*." She was much more than "an exquisite morsel" with "a seductive little face." That was obvious. But it was also true that she was not exactly a furious lioness, either. So, then, who the hell was she?

She now realized that, in seeking to defeat Gabby, she had started down a bad path, one that would never lead to the sort of accomplishment she felt was worthy of her. No, even if she had defeated Gabby and taken all her money, she still would have somehow been a failure. At least, that is how she appreciated it now.

Somehow the prince had shown her this. There was some principle that united Gabby and the prince, as if they were acting together on the same silver screen, or perhaps they were in separate movies, but the pianist played the exact same accompaniment to each screening.

No matter how they were connected, Victorine had escaped the allure of their tune. Injury, gambling losses, confinement to the Hôtel de l'Hérmitage, and listening to the prince had made it sound empty. She looked back and recalled herself before her crash and her losses, and she saw something that, superficially, looked very attractive; on closer inspection it was obviously false.

She thought of all those professional studio photos that she and all the other racers had posed for in the studio of Jules Beau. Yes, magnificent photos. Professional. But the racers sat astride bicycles which had been secretly supported and suspended by a wire, a thread as thin as gossamer, which the camera would never be able to pick up. These shots created the illusion of action, but, in reality, the subject of each portrait sat completely still. Photography seemed destined to tell this sort of lie, taking the action out of the world and fixing it into a framed image. Only, in Jules Beau's studio they seized the action even before the lens was exposed. A double cheat. It is the viewer of the photograph who puts the racer in motion, using imagination or some other principle to fill the gaps, thereby seeing more than is actually there.

It was almost impossible to photograph someone riding on an indoor track: the image would necessarily be blurry. She remembered M. Beau discussing the matter: "If it's taken outside the *atelier*, the photo won't have any 'pluck,'" he complained, using the English word. What is it, this pluck? English journalists use this word all the time when describing a *coureuse's* boldness: "Look at that one! She rides with such pluck!" "She spurted off pluckily!" "The plucky little girl from Reims." What could that possibly have in common with M. Beau's photos? A photo of real pluck would be a fuzzy, stretchy mess.

There was another thing that became clear after the prince's disappearance: Victorine was losing her patience with Sophie. This old nanny didn't know when to administer the medicine. She didn't really understand how to clean or comfort. Sophie's suggestion for dealing with her period, when it finally arose, was outrageous. A *coureuse* knows more about such things than a post-menopausal hag who has never ridden a bicycle in her life. No, Sophie was not a real nurse, whatever that might look like. How could one person be so independent and so dependent at the same time? Sophie, a small French island adrift in the great Russian Imperial Sea, floating that way—for decades. It was shocking: not a single intimate connection to call her own, and yet she was always attending to others' interests, wants and needs. It was repulsive and yet somehow also impressive.

"You must be satisfied. Prince Shirinskii-Shikhmatov read from the papers, as you requested. And?"

Victorine's face looked blank.

"As I suspected, 'All that glisters is not gold,'" she said in English. "At any rate, today I decided to read you more Pouchkine. Based on your preferences last time, with undertakers and ghosts, I think this is the best choice for you," and Sophie started reading *The Bronze Horseman* to Victorine.

The story was all confusion, no straight line to the end. It told one truth then another, first praising Peter I, then clearly casting judgement upon him. The tsar is a hero, the creator of a majestic city and the great victor of a war with Sweden, but by placing his capital on a marshy floodplain, he defies nature and exposes his citizens to needless suffering and floods, just because he wants to flex his imperial muscle and connect Russia to Europe.

The *poème* becomes much more interesting when it describes the flood. The river broils and throbs like a feverish and bedridden patient. It flails and jumps on the riverbed of primordial mud. When the river finally pours through the windows, breaking in like a thief, it is a ghastly and terrifying nightmare. It uproots trees, tears down bridges, and wipes away all the wooden buildings in its reach. It loosens the soil, soaking and inundating it, so that the cemetery vomits up its residents; coffins sail and bob down the city streets on the wind and waves where once there had been horses. If only it could have been a human power, my goodness, wouldn't that be something! But, then, even Alexander I, sitting on the balcony of his verdigris palace, an abundant island in the middle of the Baltic Sea, is forced to proclaim "Not even kings can defy the elements of God."

So, the *poème* is about a flood, emperors, empires and subjects, one subject in particular, a little mediocrity named Eugène. He takes refuge at the foot of a statue of a marble lion. It stands on a pedestal high enough for Eugène to escape the churning waters. There he waits until the flood subsides. All he can think about is his Parasha. And why not? He wants to marry her.

Is she still living? Has she been swept away in the deluge?

Later, when the flood drains away, Eugène wanders the city until he finally returns to the spot where his beloved Parasha's house once stood. It has been entirely swept away. He assumes the worst, and he is correct to do so.

Eugène goes mad and wanders the city, homeless, for a year. One day, he by chance returns to the marble lion that saved his life. Instantly, he is transported back to all the memories of the flood and the days he spent huddled around the lion's paws thinking about his poor Parasha. Nearby stands the famous statue of Peter the Great by Falconet. The emperor sits on a rearing horse as it tramples a giant snake. The statue is gargantuan. It stands atop the so-called "Thunder Stone," the biggest monolith in the world. Eugène approaches the bronze horseman, makes a very disrespectful gesture and says, "Hey you! Wonder-worker! I'll show you!"

As Eugène turns to run away, it seems that the bronze statue turns its head and shoots its blazing glare after him. He runs and runs. He swears he can hear the metallic clang of the horse's hooves hitting the cobblestones behind him. He runs faster still, not daring to look behind him. He runs and runs until he cannot run anymore.

From that moment, whenever Eugène comes near the statue, he turns and goes some other way. He continues his rootless existence for some time, until, before long, the poor man's corpse is found on a desolate island on the outskirts of the city.

"You know," Sophie continued, "when Pouchkine wrote of the Neva, he did not want to boast about its power. Nature will follow its own prerogative; only a tsar could carry his throne and his entire people to a land of swamps and floods and mosquitoes. One man moved an entire empire, not by laws, not by agreement, but by his own will. The Neva is not the monster of his story; the monster is autocracy and its mane is empire. They are the reasons for Eugène's horrifying loss. There is nothing wrong with this place, so long as it is the home for carp and herons and perhaps a Finnish fishing village, and not a capital city."

"But it doesn't make any sense."

"What do you mean, 'doesn't make any sense'? Of course it makes sense."

"Eugène is the victim of a flood. Why is the poet making such a big deal out of it? Is he asking us to feel resentment on Eugène's behalf? You cannot resent something you cannot defeat. That's madness, no?"

Victorine felt very little sympathy. Who asked Eugène to come to St. Petersburg? Surely, he knew it was prone to flooding here. Why not go to Moscow instead? He took on risk not only for himself, but also for his fiancée and any children they might have had. Had he been solitary, then be my guest. Do what you want. But that was not the case. Others are going to suffer because of your dreams.

But Sophie would not accept Victorine's objections: "This little man, this Eugène, he wants to marry Parasha. It will be hard for him, of course, being so poor and so cut off from his social roots. But can you blame him for hoping to build a little sanctuary for himself and his wife after a life of struggle? Eugène is not some hero. His wants are simple. Why deprive him? Were Eugène alive today, perhaps he would be what the Russians call a *tchastnik*, a small shop-keeper—independent, financially vulnerable because he assumes all risk. He ekes out a meagre existence on the fringes of society, hoping to make his way from the outside. He has no connections. He has no tradition. He is a completely new man! He scrapes to get by, hoping against hope to find stability, nothing more. He is reaching, reaching not for the divine or the sacred. What can such things mean to a man who longs only for comfort and normalcy? No, Eugène is the new myth.

"But who will defend him? Will you? No, not you! Why not? Because you ride a bicycle! The human suffering that has been perpetuated just so that you can ride in circles inside a horsey manège in February. The miners who dig up your metal, the workers who put it all together. What about the rubber for your tires? Who collects all that? How much horror is perpetrated just so that you can hold your cloistered races? But you wouldn't care about any of that would you? You, *ma femme de manière garçonnière* with a bicycle! The world is just a big fight for you, *non*? Always trying to see who is first, fastest, best, not caring about the rest, as if you can take Darwin, spin him in circles around your foolish track, and, then, when you are done, hold him up as the standard of virtue."

"There is no harm in racing. I'm allowed to develop myself, my skills."

"Develop yourself… How can you pretend to climb to the top of a ladder (and such a strange and idiotic ladder, too) without asking why the world is filled with so much inequality? A person, better than you, would hurl herself to the ground, begging the earth for forgiveness, rather than reaching for any height if attaining it also meant stepping on the skulls and throats of others."

"What are you talking about? I'm not some princess. I come from a ruined family too, only my father didn't have a flood as an excuse. No, we suffered because of his recklessness. If he's still alive, he's still repaying his debts!"

"But in that case, you ought to know better! You are in France. You can do things. Join a cause. Do you know what it means to join a cause in this country? Exile! Imprisonment! Death! Surely you know the Russians have already assassinated one tsar. And why not!? Do you know what happened at the last coronation, just a few months ago? Why, they were in Moscow, celebrating. Then there was a panic, and then there was a stampede. Thousands were trampled to death, not by horses, but by each other. They asked Nicholas to postpone the coronation, but he proceeded anyways. What a shame that was! And what a dark portent! How can a tsar begin to rule under such a horrible sign? Things like this happen and yet you still want to ride a bicycle!?"

Victorine made to get up out of bed. The bruises were still very tender and her stitches felt like they might tear. It wasn't fair to be forced to listen to Pouchkine and then to get this unsolicited opinion from an old, dried-up, tripe-faced hag.

"Please stay in bed. You are unwell. Besides, I'm not finished talking to you. That's right. There is more.

"I'm sure you imagine you are some exceptionally independent human being. You have thrown your bonnet under the windmill, as the saying goes. A woman—yes. Exceptional freedom you have—yes. I mean, true, you're a little tied down at the moment, yes, but once you recuperate it will be back on the track for you. And then you'll be allowed to think that you enjoy more freedom than almost everyone. More than most men? More than the prince? More than the tsar? Hmm?

"But don't you feel, sometimes," added Sophie, "that you are just a pawn. After all, you compete under the control of the men who organize your races. And these men have designs, goals that you unwittingly help them accomplish. Don't you know that the prince and his partner used your races to advance their investments, to ship bicycles in from Warsaw and to sell them at their proposed bicycle shop on Nevskii Prospect? Surely you at least appreciate that the men hold gambling pools on you?

"You say you're developing yourself! *Non, ma chérie!* Not at all! Those wheels look like spiders' webs to me, and the frames look like gallows. You do not drive your own wheels but are trapped within the ones they make for you."

It was impossible to listen anymore. It was time to go home. Despite the pain, Victorine got out of bed, and, as she got up on her feet, she saw on Sophie's lap, in familiar French, *Les oeuvres choisies de A.S. Pouchkine.** That witch was not some virtuoso translator after all.

"What's this? You *tricheuse*!† I don't need you to read to me if it's in French. The stitches are on my belly, not across my eyes!"

Sophie took on a surprised and almost affronted air: "I didn't think you could ..."

"I'm leaving! Right away!"

"Mlle. Reillo, I am sorry for upsetting you. It is my intention to help you. I am very concerned for you, and I do earnestly hope that you recover quickly, because you really must regain your health as soon as possible." And here Sophie suddenly became very quiet and serious: "My aim in reading this *poème* was not to irritate you, though it was to provoke you. I do want you to get out of bed, I do want you to get out of this city, but you must wait. As soon as you are ready..."

"I'm ready now..." She went through her chest, got out her dress, overcoat and chapeau. She had to move gingerly, but she also worked methodically.

"This story is fantastical, but it is also true," continued Sophie. "There really are floods here. They say this city is damned. Peter the Great fought with a god and won, yes. He opened his Russian window to the west. But his victory was temporary and incomplete; the god comes back from time to time to remind us that he will claim the ultimate victory. Oh, the floods I have witnessed! I'm certain that one day this city will lie at the bottom of the Baltic Sea! It must happen. This city is doomed. It is only a matter of time. You must return to Paris as soon as you can!

"But, when you do return, for the love of all that is good in this world, use your money and freedom to do work that is righteous and correct. Do not waste your youth, your strength, or your health on these damned races!"

---

* *The Selected Works of A.S. Pushkin.*

† "cheat"

Finally, Victorine was dressed. She felt her reticule around her neck. She was in such a state that she completely forgot: she had given everything to Gabrielle.

"I don't have any money."

"What? How can that be possible, Mlle. Reillo?"

"My 'Zimmy.' Where is it?"

"Your what?"

"My *bécane*. I must exchange it for some money. Where is it?"

"I'm sure that I don't know! How on earth would I?" This was not a rhetorical question. "But, really, you are being radically precipitous. Sit down, please. It goes without saying that I shall arrange for some funds to be brought to you, but not yet. Can't you see that you have more recovering to do?"

But Victorine was already out the door and making her way down the stairs. She moved with a strange haste, punctuated, at times, by pauses brought on by the pain.

She approached the front desk, requested that her "Zimmy" be brought, and she enquired where the nearest pawnbroker was to be found.

XII

The hotel manager bought Victorine's bicycle. He did not stint her; she had plenty of money to get home.

As for the train, it really was true that it was less than a five-minute walk from the hotel. But she had to wait five hours before the train departed.

The train ride was long and uncomfortable. She didn't have any of Gabby's dime novels to read. She didn't miss them, however, because she had other things on her mind.

Like that *Bronze Horseman*. What on earth had Sophie read to her? Unbelievable! And how could she read into it the way she did? No, it wasn't Eugène that made one think. It was Peter the Great. He moved his city in order to—what did Sophie say? —to "open a window." Instead, all he got for his trouble were floods and an ungrateful poet. Perhaps he should have made do with Moscow, just accepted it for what it was and made it better. Or maybe he should have conquered more and better land rather than stopping at the Baltic. In any case, it was obvious that Peter the Great picked a foolish place to settle.

There was a flood in St. Petersburg in 1897. Sophie did not drown, but the prince declared bankruptcy and had to sponge off his brother. This had obvious consequences for Sophie: she had to return to France. It also had consequences for Colonel Gelmersen who served his few remaining days in Count Sheremetiev's fire brigade.

Journal des Sports reported that Victorine was already racing again by April of 1897. Unfortunately, she lost her sponsorship deal with Nimrod. They refused to believe her story about losing her "Zimmy" in transit. Luckily, she struck a new sponsorship deal with Phébus, a proper French company, who spared no amount of ink bragging about all her successes in Russia.

E. Ollier paid her membership dues up until 1899. She still declared "Victorine Reillo" as her pseudonym. After that, both Ollier and Reillo disappear from the journalistic record forever.

CHAPTER FOUR

Tessie Reynolds and the Hundred-and-Twenty-Mile Record

Brighton-London-Brighton, 10 September 1893

The morning was damp and cool with a wizened mist, the leaves hung heavily and were already starting to turn colour, and the sixteen-year-old Tessie Reynolds set out from the Brighton Aquarium. It was 5:00 am. Right from the first pedal stroke, she moved quickly: it looked like she was going downhill, all the time.

Her goal was simple: ride all the way to Hyde Park in London, turn around and come back to the start as fast as possible. One-hundred-and-twenty miles. It was a well-used route, serving as the control whenever an English athlete wanted to establish a new record. Despite no shortage of attempts, Sherland's 1890 time of nine hours and nineteen minutes still stood firmly in place. It was the beacon. No other contender had yet extinguished it; Tessie intended to douse it with her perspiration.

Spring and summer had been spent in training at the Preston Park velodrome with her father, RJ Reynolds. Do laps at every opportunity. Learn the comfort of discomfort. Discuss your diet. Most important of all, just ride.

17. Tessie Reynolds

Really, RJ had been preparing her for this event for her entire life. He had a passion for all forms of athleticism; it would have been unthinkable not to share his passion with Tessie. He taught her how to box, how to fence and how to ride a bicycle. He also taught her about the business and community of cycling. He was a bicycle dealer, he invigilated races, he was the Secretary of the Brighton Cycling Club, and he was a member of the National Cycling Union. He and his wife transformed their home into a destination for cycling tourists, offering accommodation, food and refreshment, repairs and maps. Her father knew all about the cycling world.

And so he also knew his daughter's ride would be received with ridicule. Tessie needed protection. If she was going to take on the record, there was a way to go about it. There had to be adjudicators at every control and there had to be pacers to accompany Tessie along the way. Don't give anyone an excuse or a pretext to contest the result just because it was smashed by a teenaged girl.

By 9:13 am, she was already in Hyde Park. She turned around and didn't stop until the control in Smitham Bottom. Her father just missed her, but he caught the train to Three Bridges and met her at the next control in Crawley. After that, she was on her own until Brighton: the control in Hickstead was just too far from the train line.

She made it back to the Brighton Aquarium by 1:38pm. Eight hours and thirty-eight minutes, completely smashing Sherland's record by forty-one minutes. No wonder the entire morning went by in a flash.

The reaction in the press was negative. First, no one took her accomplishment seriously. A woman's record, or more correctly a girl's, was nothing more than a novelty. No formal club or organization could acknowledge or approve it, despite her father's precautions.

Far more ink was spilled on the subject of Tessie's attire, a sort of Norfolk jacket with very long pockets to conceal the thighs made in Worstead suiting arranged atop of matching bloomers. Beneath she wore a readymade white cotton blouse. *Cycling Magazine* accused the outfit of "scantiness" and called Tessie's ride a "lamentable incident":

> Every wheelman who has managed to maintain a belief
> in the innate modesty and sense of becomingness in the
> opposite sex, will hear with real pain, not unmixed with
> disgust, of what we will call a lamentable incident that
> took place on the Brighton road early last Sunday.

Another journal called Tessie and her outfit nothing but "a caricature of the sweetest and best half of humanity."

But there were other voices in the liberal press that supported her. George Lacy Hillier wrote an article about her in *Bicycling News*. He congratulated her for abandoning ordinary dress and having the courage to wear rationals, calling her "the stormy petrel heralding the storm of revolt against the petticoat," who "has ridden in a costume suited to cycling." He concluded, "so long as a lady can ride well and gracefully I see no objection at all to the adoption by her of a suitable, eminently rational, and particularly safe costume, which relieves her once and for all of the flapping and dangerous skirt…" The first issues of *The Lady Cyclist* similarly applauded Reynold's choice of dress:

> By her ride, and the extraordinary correspondence it has
> provoked, together with the reproduction of her photo-
> graph throughout the country, Miss Reynolds has accom-
> plished more in three weeks in stirring up opinion about
> ladies' rational dress than could otherwise have been
> achieved in as many years.

Many women admired her outfit and asked her to share the pattern. There are so few examples of viable athletic attire for women. Tessie had to confess that she had no pattern to share. She just made her outfit to her own needs.

All the storm in the press didn't matter one way or another. The detractors missed the point as much as the proponents. Attack or support the outfit. Who cares? Ignore the rightfully-earned record? Well, truth be told, that one did sting a little. But everyone knows the truth, whether they acknowledge it or not.

No, the main thing was being such a huge help. Maybe now, with all this publicity, the family can rise up above the stormy fray of the daily struggle and start to live a little.

NOTES

INTRODUCTION: WOMEN RACERS AND THE GREAT BICYCLE CRAZE OF THE 1890S

The Rover Safety. See David V. Herlihy, *Bicycle: The History* (Yale UP, 2006), 225.

The bicycle craze of the 1890s: It is not possible, here, to provide a complete bibliography on the importance the bicycle's importance during the 1890s, but some key texts are Margaret Guroff, *The Mechanical Horse: How the Bicycle Reshaped American Life* (U of Texas P, 2016), Herlihy, *Bicycle: The History*, William Manners, *Revolution: How the Bicycle Reinvented Modern Britain* (Duckworth, 2019), Glen Norcliffe, *The Ride to Modernity: The Bicycle in Canada, 1869-1900* (U of Toronto P, 2001), and Robert A. Smith, *A Social History of the Bicycle* (American Heritage Press, 1972).

Susan B. Anthony's letter to the editor of *Sidepaths*. Quoted in Lynn Sherr, *Failure is Impossible: Susan B. Anthony in Her Own Words* (Times Books, 1995), 277.

Frances E. Willard. See Frances E. Willard, *Let Something Good Be Said* Eds. Amy R. Slagell, Carolyn De Swarte Gifford. (U of Illinois P, 2007). My book takes inspiration from the title of Willard's book, *A Wheel within a Wheel*.

"[Women's cycling in the 1890s] is as well established as it is well-documented." Again, it is impossible to cite all the relevant literature here, but the following titles offer a decent survey: Ann-Katrin Ebert, "Liberating Technologies? Of Bicycles, Balance, and 'The New Woman,'" *Icon* 16 (2010): 25-52, Ellen Gruber Garvery, "Reframing the Bicycle: Advertising-Supported Magazines and Scorching Women," *American Quarterly* 47.1 (1995): 66-101, Kat Jungnickel, *Bikes and Bloomers: Victorian Women Inventors and their Extraordinary Cycle Wear* (MIT Press, 2018), Patricia Marks, *Bicycles, Bangs and Bloomers: The New Woman in the Popular Press* (U of Kentucky P, 1990), Hannah Ross, *Revolutions: How Women Changed the World on Two Wheels* (Plume, 2020), and Anita Rush, "The Bicycle Boom of the Gay Nineties: A Reassessment," *Material Culture Review* 18 (1983): 1-12.

Bourgeois women and cycling. I gratefully acknowledge the generosity of Phillip Gordon Mackintosh of Brock University for sharing his research on this subject, see his "A Bourgeois Geography of Domestic Cycling," *Journal of Historical Sociology* 20.1/2 (2007): 126-157; "Flâneurie on Bicycles: Acquiescence to Women in Public in the 1890s," *The Canadian Geographer* 50.1 (2006): 17-37.

Illustration of the San Jose Women's Cycling Club. By the author 2022. Source image: "A Group of the Ladies' Cycling Club of San Jose" *The San Francisco Call* (1 June 1895): 9.

The lower social status of the racers. I used several sources to fill my knowledge gaps on the racers' origins: on seamstresses, see Wendy Gamber, *The Female Economy: The Millinery and Dressmaking Trades, 1860-1930.* (U of Illinois P, 1997), Christina Walkley, *Ghost in the Looking Glass: The Victorian Seamstress.* (Peter Own Ltd., 1981); on working-class women more generally, see Nan Enstad, *Ladies of Labor, Girls of Adventure* (Columbia UP, 1999), and Kathy Peiss, *Cheap Amusements: Working Women and Leisure in Turn-of-the-Century New York.* (Temple UP, 1986).

"The Cult of True Womanhood." Barbara Welter, "The Cult of True Womanhood: 1820-1860," *American Quarterly* 18.2 (1966): 151-174.

"It is impossible to be domestic…" See Christine Stansell, *City of Women: Sex and Class in New York, 1789-1860.* (Alfred A. Knopf, 1986).

"It is impossible to be pure…" See Ruth Rosen, *The Lost Sisterhood: Prostitution in America, 1900-1918.* (Johns Hopkins UP, 1982), and Stansell, *City of Women.*

"Character" and "personality": See Warren E. Susman, "Personality and the Making of Twentieth-Century Culture," *Culture as History: The Transformation of American Society in the Twentieth Century.* (Pantheon, 1984), 271-286.

The League of American Wheelmen: Philip P. Mason, *The League of American Wheelmen and the Good-Roads Movement, 1880-1905.* Diss., U of Michigan, 1957.

"…the men who organized these events regarded their guests as pawns…" I follow Betsy Wearing's discussion about men's relationship to sport and leisure as being determined primarily by "functionalism": see Wearing, *Leisure and Feminist Theory* (SAGE, 1999), 20-21; see also Michael S. Kimmel, *Manhood in America: A Cultural History* (Oxford UP, 2017).

"There were intrinsic rewards to racing…" Here I draw on discussions of symbolic interactionism. See, for example, Norman Denzin, *Symbolic Interactionism and Cultural Studies* (Oxford UP, 1992), and Wearing, *Leisure and Feminist Theory*, 41-2.

"…demands of a higher order." I am deeply indebted to Jonathan Lear and his definition of irony in helping me to articulate my characters, their dilemmas and their solutions. See his *A Case for Irony* (Harvard UP, 2011).

"…temper their aspirations with the cold facts of reality." I share with Mary Harrington an interest in acknowledging the limits on human agency despite the benefits of technology: see her *Feminism Against Progress* (Regnery, 2023).

CHAPTER ONE: THE ROYAL AQUARIUM

The Royal Aquarium was once located steps away from Westminster Abbey in London. See John Murchison Munro, *The Royal Aquarium: Failure of a Victorian Compromise* (American University of Beirut, 1971).

"The Royal Aquarium used to have fish…" Munro, *The Royal Aquarium*, 12; "The Whale in the Aquarium," *Daily News* (29 Sep. 1877): 6.

"…gentlemen started luring girls…" Munro, *The Royal Aquarium*, 53.

"The Human Horse…" "Entertainment Items," *The Observer* (17 Nov. 1895): 3; "The Royal Aquarium: Always a Remarkable Programme," *The Graphic: An Illustrated Weekly Newspaper* (23 Nov. 1895): 5.

"And then there is the sham music hall…" Munro, *The Royal Aquarium*, 62-4.

"This Ladies' Race is the crest of a wave…" See Sheila Hanlon, "Ladies' Cycle Races at the Royal Aquarium: A Late Victorian Sporting Spectacle." *Sheila Hanlon/Historian/ Women's Cycling.* 26 January 2015, and Mike Fishpool, "The Wheeling Wonders of London: The Lady Cyclists of the Royal Aquarium's First Professional Women's Cycling Tournament." *Playing Pasts: The Online Magazine for Sport & Leisure History.* 25 May 2020.

"…carrier wave…" Norcliffe, *The Ride to Modernity* 22.

"One of them is particularly famous—Mlle. Lisette….Mlle. Victorine Reillo is another big name." "Ladies' Bicycle Races," *Birmingham Daily Gazette* (19 Nov. 1895): 6.

"appallingly garrulous" *Leeds Mercury* (20 Nov. 1895): 5.

"It is bizarre to hear hoarse and husky female French voices…" *Derby Daily Telegraph* (23 Nov. 1895): 2.

"They blow kisses…" "Ladies' Cycling Race," *Manchester Evening News* (20 Nov. 1895): 3.

"Hélène Dutrieux…Fanouche Vautro…" "Lady Cyclists at the Westminster Aquarium," *Guardian* (19 Nov. 1895): 8; *Birmingham Daily Gazette* (19 Nov. 1895): 4.

"La corde, nom de dieu..." *Derby Telegraph* (23 Nov. 1895): 2.

Illustration of Hélène Dutrieux. By the author 2023. Source: photo by Henry R. Gibbs "Women Cyclists at the Agricultural Hall," *The Sketch* (8 Apr. 1896): 453. To learn more about Hélène Dutrieux, see Gunter Segers, *Hélène Dutrieu: The Amazing Life of the Girl Sparrow Hawk.* (Les Iles, 2023).

"Now you Frenchies keep to the side..." *Derby Daily Telegraph* (23 Nov. 1895): 2.

"Reillo and Solange are temporarily disqualified..." "Ladies' Cycling Race," *Manchester Evening News* (20 Nov. 1895): 3; "Ladies' Cycling Race," *Daily Telegraph* (20 Nov. 1895): 8; "Wheeler's Column," *The People* (24 Nov. 1895): 4.

"The audience finds her penalty entirely deserved..." *Chesham Examiner* (29 Nov. 1895): 6.

"Attendance is consistently 'immense'..." *Gloucestershire Echo* (22 Nov. 1895): 3.; "Cycling Gossip," *Weekly Dispatch* (24 Nov. 1895): 7.

"... 'lordly guinea'..." and **"... 'humble shilling'..."** "The Lady Cyclists at the Aquarium," *Westminster Budget* (29 Nov. 1895): 23.

"Prince Francis of Teck..." *Devon and Exeter Gazette* (20 Nov. 1895): 3.; "Ladies' Bicycle Races," *The People* (24 Nov. 1895): 16.

"a 'well-known sporting duke'..." "At the Aquarium," *Nottingham Evening Post* (26 Nov. 1895): 2.

"They are grooms in front of a great white veil." This chapter's preoccupation with the audience (and its failure to realize the true significance of this event) is inspired, in part, by my reading of Jacques Rancière's *The Emancipated Spectator* (Verso, 2009), 1-23.

"the spice of peril in a performance." "Our London Letter," *Wealdstone, Harrow and Wembley Observer* (29 Nov. 1895): 2.

"The tumbles are so numerous and shocking..." "Lady Cyclists at the Westminster Aquarium," *Guardian* (19 Nov. 1895): 8.

"The contest between lady cyclists at the Aquarium seems to be regarded rather as an amusement than a genuine race..." *Manchester Evening News* (20 Nov. 1895): 2.

"Whether their object is to gain notoriety..." "Women's Activities by an Active Woman," *Western Morning News* (22 Nov. 1895): 7.

"The spectator is divided between a profound concern..." *Leeds Mercury* (20 Nov. 1895): 5.

"It is doubtful whether women are consulting their own dignity..." "Outlook in the City." – Look out! *Weekly Dispatch* (24 Nov. 1895): 11.

"If the prohibitive taint of hopeless vulgarity..." *Retford and Worksop and North Notts Advertiser* (23 Nov. 1895): 8.

"A good many people, no doubt, mindful only of the race athletically..." *Peterborough and Hunts Standard* (23 Nov. 1895): 5.

"...a society for the prevention of cruelty to female riders." *The People* (24 Nov. 1895): 4.

"These Amazons of the wheel..." *Cambria Daily Leader* (28 Nov. 1895): 2.

"The women constitute a show that attracts." "Whirling on the Wheel: Professionals of the Feminine Gender," *Pall Mall Gazette* (29 Nov. 1895): 11.

"They call such features 'bicycle face'..." Newspapers and various professionals of the day discussed *bicycle face* to express anxiety about women displaying physical exertion in public. See, for example, Margaret Guroff, *The Mechanical Horse*, 46.

"...the same nameless but eternal mystery." A variation on some lines in Joseph Conrad's *Heart of Darkness* (1899).

"The racers wear 'go-as-you-please'..." *Daily News* (19 November 1895): 5.

"Miss Hutton wears tight satin breeches..." *Guardian* (2 Dec. 1895): 6.

"Lisette gets her silk *tricolore* shoulder sash..." Mike Fishpool, "The Wheeling Wonders of London."

"The French wear their hair in plain 'bobs." *Berrow's Worcester Journal*, (23 Nov. 1895): 5, quoted in Fishpool, "The Wheeling Wonders of London"; "Lady Cyclists," *Yorkshire Herald and the York Herald* (25 Nov. 1895): 6.

"electric blue" *Daily News* (19 Nov. 1895): 5.

"The press claims that the competitors 'have donned male habiliments'..." *Leeds Mercury* (20 Nov. 1895): 5.

"...did not even take the trouble to have the upper parts of their breeches baggy." "Our London Letter," *Wealdstone, Harrow and Wembley Observer* (29 Nov. 1895): 2.

Illustration of Nellie Hutton. By the author 2023. Source: *Six Day Cycle Races*: http://sixday.org.uk/html/19c_female_riders.html

"There are some very taking costumes..." *North Star* (20 Nov. 1895): 3.

"There can be no exception to the costumes worn..." "Lady Cyclist Competition, Its Value," *Coventry Herald and Free Press* (29 Nov. 1895): 3.

"...they ask questions; not all of them are stupid." The entire exchange that follows can be found in "Whirling on the wheel," *Pall Mall Gazette* (19 Nov. 1895): 11.

To learn more about **Miss Rosina Lane**, see Fishpool, "The Wheeling Wonders of London"; Jungnickel, *Bikes and Bloomers*, 133-5.

"The appearance of the wife of a Chelsea tradesman in a race..." "Chelsea Gossip," *West London Press, Westminster and Chelsea News* (29 Nov. 1895): 5.

Illustration of Rosina Lane. By the author, 2021. Source: photo by Messieurs Russel & Sons, "The Lady Cyclists at the Aquarium," *The Sketch* (27 Nov. 1895): 233.

"The total accumulated race time was twenty-two-and-a-half hours." "The Lady Cyclists," *Northern Echo* (26 Nov. 1895): 3.

"...the suggestion that they were only paste." "Chelsea Gossip," *West London Press, Westminster and Chelsea News* (29 Nov. 1895): 5.

"Tea and toast have not figured largely upon the bills..." "Whirling on the wheel: Professionals of the Feminine Gender," *Pall Mall Gazette* (19 Nov. 1895): 11.

"Harwood had actually gained four pounds during the race." "Chelsea Gossip," *West London Press, Westminster and Chelsea News* (29 Nov. 1895): 5.

"Harwood...got to keep her Atlas bicycle and Lane got a deal with the Swift Cyclery Co..." "Ladies Cycling Race," *Middlesex and Buckinghamshire Advertiser, Etc.* (23 Nov. 1895): 4.

"Lisette got a deal with the Simpson Chain Company..." "Fifty Miles an Hour on a Bike," *The Sketch* (8 Jan. 1896): 545.

"One man... created new purses to award them out of his own pocket." "Whirling on the wheel: Professionals of the Feminine Gender," *Pall Mall Gazette* (19 Nov. 1895): 11.

Illustration of Victorine Reillo. By the author, 2023. Source: photo by Messieurs Russel & Sons, "The Lady Cyclists at the Aquarium," *The Sketch* (27 Nov. 1895): 233.

"No, the *rosbif* should have asked us how to build a track..." There were other complaints about the track size: see "Cycling Gossip" *The Weekly Dispatch* (24 November 1895): 7; and *The Coleshill Chronicle* (23 November 1895): 8.

Illustration of the Exterior of the Royal Aquarium. By the author, 2023.

CHAPTER TWO: THE FESTIVAL OF FIRE

Illustration of the Father of the Waters. By the author, 2023. Source: A Pillsbury commercial of 1912, employed anachronistically. Found in *The Bellman* (12 Mar. 1912): rear cover; also, see "Spiritual Power to Industrial Might: 12,000 Years of St. Anthony Falls," *Minnesota History* (Spring/Summer 2003): 269.

"There was that skinny bellhop…" Isabel Best, *Queens of Pain: Legends & Rebels of Cycling* (Rapha, 2018), 18.

"Swede Town." See Ulf Beijbom, "Chicago's 'Swede Town'—Gone but not Forgotten," *Swedish Pioneer Historical Society* 15.4 (1964): 144.

"A pair of sheep and a mended roof are better than wandering." *Hávamál: The Sayings of the Vikings.* trans. Björn Jónasson (Gudrun Publishing, 2018), 51.

For biographical details about **Tillie Anderson**, I have depended on Roger Gilles's amazing book, *Women on the Move: The Forgotten Era of Women's Bicycle Racing* (U of Nebraska P, 2018).

Tillie Anderson vs. Reverend Moody: Gilles, *Women on the Move*, 119-21; "Rev. Dwight L. Moody Discovers Tillie Anderson" *The St. Louis Republic* (12 December 1897).

"They're together at the World's Columbian Exposition in 1893." James Gilbert, *Perfect Cities: Chicago's Utopias of 1893* (U of Chicago P, 1991); Neil Harris, "Great American Fairs and American Cities: The Role of Chicago's Columbian Exposition," in *Cultural Excursions* (U of Chicago P, 1990), 111-31; Robert Rydell, "The Chicago World's Columbian Exposition of 1893," in *All the World's a Fair* (U of Chicago P, 1987), 38-71; Alan Trachtenberg, *The Incorporation of America* (Macmillan, 1982).

The Fanny Darling interview: "Bicycle Racing Transforms Lovely Woman from a Pale Beauty into a Perfect Fright," *St. Louis Post-Dispatch* (5 Dec. 1897): 16; Gilles, *Women on the Move*, 144-7.

"A few days later, a doctor, a reporter and an illustrator showed up at the Belvedere Hotel…" Gilles, *Women on the Move*, 139.

"William Edwin Haskell had been in court since mid-December." "State vs. Haskell. Jury Renders a Verdict of Not Guilty in the Case," *Minneapolis Star Tribune* (5 Feb. 1898): 7.

"Samuel Hill…had sold a defunct company's bonds for ten cents on the dollar…" John E. Tuhy, *Sam Hill: The Prince of Castle Nowhere* (Timbre Press, 1983), 40.

"We, the jury, find the defendant William E. Haskell, not guilty…" "State vs. Haskell. Jury Renders a Verdict of Not Guilty in the Case," *Minneapolis Star Tribune* (5 Feb. 1898): 7.

"…the muckraking journalism of Lincoln Steffens…" Lincoln Steffens, "The Shame of Minneapolis," *McClure's Magazine* XX (3 Jan. 1903): 227-39.

"*Forty Years in the Wilderness.*" Tuhy, *Sam Hill*, 37-40.

"One correspondent watched a young Cuban mother die…" Stephen Kinzer, *The True Flag: Theodore Roosevelt, Mark Twain, and the Birth of American Empire* (Henry Holt and Co., 2017).

"The United States is on the verge of a crisis…" "Much War Talk," *Minneapolis Daily Times* (21 Mar. 1898): 1.

"…even though 'nobody outside a lunatic asylum' actually believed that Spain was responsible…" Joseph Pulitzer, of the famed Pulitzer prize, coined this phrase when referring to the sinking of the Maine.

"…Roosevelt countered with a big smile, 'I clipped him in the left breast as he turned.'" Stephen Kinzer, *The True Flag*.

"It wasn't the bald eagle's talons digging into the Philippines or Cuba…" Mark Twain came up with the image of the eagle's talons as metaphor for American imperialistic war and with the image of miniature constitutions floating at great distances away from the continental US. *New York Herald* (15 Oct. 1900).

"…sources that could not be described as patriotic or loyal to the great American flag." This is a verbatim quote from Theodore Roosevelt.

"capability made it a scientific necessity": For an introduction to the origin and ideas of social Darwinism, I referred to Mike Hawkins' *Social Darwinism in European and American Thought, 1860-1945* (Cambridge UP, 1997).

"There was that dandy one of the young private with three skulls." Krystle Stricklin, "With a Skull in Each Hand: Boneyard Photography in the American Empire after 1898," in *Imperial Islands: Art, Architecture, and Visual Experience in the US Insular Empire after 1898*, ed. Joseph R. Hartman (U of Hawaii P, 2021), 62.

"Picture a great human skull with missing teeth encircled by a ring of fire." *The Worthington Advance* (1 Sep. 1898): 8.

Illustration of the Fire Festival Admission Button. By the author, 2023. Source: https://www.worthpoint.com/worthopedia/festival-fire-1898-minneapolis-1997390398

"Fire Festival' is the word on every tongue..." "Now for the fun. Fire Festival Week has at last arrived," *Minneapolis Daily Times* (4 Sep. 1898): 6.

Edwin Haskell and *The Boston Herald*. Edwin A. Perry, *The Boston Herald and its History*, (RM Pulsifer, 1878).

Blethen's Cowboys: Sherry A. Boswell and Lorraine McConaghy, *Raise Hell and Sell Newspapers: Alden J. Blethen and The Seattle Times* (Washington State UP, 1996); Press Club of Minneapolis, *Souvenirs and Entertainment* (1904), 23-4; 101.

"...that outlaw Jesse James." Boswell and McConaghy, *Raise Hell*, 34.

Illustration of Edwin Haskell and Associates on his Electric Carriage. By the author 2023. Source: Boswell and McConaghy, *Raise Hell*, 53.

"...location of the Minnesota State Fair..." Boswell and McConaghy, *Raise Hell*, 48.

The Industrial Exposition Building. The best source of information about the Industrial Exposition Building, its construction, its purpose and its significance, is Peter Ausenhaus's dissertation, *Civic Image and the Building of the Minneapolis Industrial Exposition* (1996).

"The manifest destiny of the young metropolitan giant..." *Minneapolis Daily Tribune* (11 Oct. 1885): 1. Quoted in Ausenhaus, *Civic Image*, 128.

President Grover Cleveland's young wife and the scandalous editorial in the *Tribune*: Boswell and McConaghy, *Raise Hell*, 50-1.

The fire at the *Tribune* headquarters: Boswell and McConaghy, *Raise Hell*, 60-3.

The Industrial Exposition vs. The State Fair: I depended on Warren E. Susman's "character" and "personality" when making these distinctions. See my introduction.

"The program is the result of an amalgamated union of brains, genius and everlasting energy." "Now for the fun. Fire Festival Week has at last arrived," *Minneapolis Daily Times* (4 Sep. 1898): 6.

Lisette: Gilles, *Women on the Move*, 205-48.

Illustration of Lisette. By the author, 2022. Source: from a photograph by Jules Beau.

Lisette's actual method of **coffee divination** differed from my presentation. See Gilles, *Women on the Move*, 213.

First Night: "Wheels Spun as Fast as Tops," *Minneapolis Daily Times* (6 Sep. 1898): 1.

Bicycle Day and "The Most Attractive Uniformed Club Composed Exclusively of Ladies...etc." *Annual Report of the Minnesota Agricultural Society, 1896* (St. Paul: Minnesota Agricultural Society, 1897), 21.

Second Night: "Whirl of Wheels Delights the Eyes," *Minneapolis Daily Times* (7 Sep. 1898): 1.

"...there was something familiar, like a ghost coming back to haunt itself." Lear, *A Case for Irony*, p. 46.

"...Officer Chamberlain shook her roughly by the shoulder." "Whirl of Wheels Delights the Eyes," *Minneapolis Daily Times* (7 Sep. 1898): 1.

Illustration of Tillie Anderson. By the author, 2021. Source: based of the photo archive of Alice Roepke, great Niece of Tillie Anderson, *Tillie Anderson Website*, http://tillieanderson.com/tillie/.

Third Night: "Girls Jockey Lisette," *Minneapolis Daily Times* (8 Sep. 1898): 1.

Fourth Night: "Little French Girl Outgeneraled at the Finish as Usual," *Minneapolis Daily Times* (9 Sep. 1898): 1.

Fifth Night: "Race Last Night Was Run Fairly but Not Without Accident," *Minneapolis Daily Times* (10 Sep. 1898): 1.

Sixth Night: "Lisette Got Second Place," *Minneapolis Daily Times* (11 Sep. 1898): 1; "What 'Dad' Moulton Says," *Minneapolis Daily Times* (11 Sep. 1898): 3.

"long song." I found the term *"chant long"* in my readings about Béla Bartók who studied the folklore and folk music of Hungary, Slovakia, Romania and other Central European lands in search of the original music of *homo sapiens*. See Ambrus Miskolczy, "Mythe et religion dans la Cantata Profana de Béla Bartók ou le mystère des fils changés en cerfs," *Hungarian Studies* 2 (2017): 163-73.

"...whirlpool and...the giant, splintered rocks." The Dakota name for St. Anthony's Falls is *Owamniyomni*, or "whirlpool." The Ojibway name is *Gichi-gakaabikaa*, or "great splintered rocks" Tom Weber, *Minneapolis: An Urban Biography* (Minnesota Historical Society, 2022), 24.

"...games of vertigo and mimicry..." This entire chapter makes use of Roger Caillois's four distinctions of play: *alea* (chance), *agon* (competition), *ilinx* (vertigo) and *mimicry* all appear in one form or another in these pages. See Caillois, *Man, Play and Games*. trans. Meyer Barash (U of Illinois P, 2001).

"...all [the flour] exploded and nearly destroyed the whole town." Airborne particles of flour are highly flammable. On 2 May 1878, a massive flour explosion occurred. It was so destructive that a third of the city's milling capacity was destroyed, and eighteen people were killed. See Weber, *Minneapolis*, 52.

"...they built so much they nearly killed the falls." Ausenhaus, *Civic Image*, 110; Lucile M. Kane, *The Falls of St. Anthony* (Minnesota Historical Society, 1987), 62-80; Weber, *Minneapolis*, 37-42.

CHAPTER THREE: THE MIKHAILOVSKII MANÈGE

Abbreviations for the Russian publications:

PG – Petersburg Gazette [Петербургская газета]

PL – Petersburg Leaflet [Петербургский листок]. Dates for the *PL* are given according to the Russian calendar and the Western calendar (in brackets)

RC – Russian Cyclist [Циклист]

"Does Mlle. Reillo have any words to convey to her readers of *Paris-Vélo*?" "L'État de Mlle. Reillo," *Paris-Vélo* (samedi 13 mars 1897): 1.; "Cyclisme," *Gil Blas* (11 mars 1897): 4.

"...a suite of the Hôtel de l'Hérmitage." This hotel was located on the corner of Nevskii Prospect and Znamenskaia Street (today Vosstainie Street). It specialized in serving cyclists. "Наброски по сезону [Sketches of the Season]," *RC* 49 (2 (14) марта 1897): 3.

"...championne du kilomètre..." *L'Écho de Rouen illustré* (5 mai 1897).

"...la meilleure des dames..." "Couriers étrangers: Angleterre, à l'Agricultural Hall," *Le Véloce-Sport* (2 avr. 1896): 18.

"...up-and-comer..." *Le Véloce-Sport* (13 mai 1897): 18. The word used in the original French is "comingwoman," (i.e. an English word). The word is not in the *OED*. I think it is intended as a complement and is the equivalent of saying Victorine is "up-and-coming."

"La gentille Reillo..." *Paris-Vélo* (15 novembre 1896): 2.

"l'amiable Reillo..." *Le Véloce-Sport* (13 mai 1897): 18.

"L'exquise Reillo..." *Le Véloce-Sport* (2 septembre 1897): 9.

"La petite Reillo..." *Le Véloce-Sport* (4 mars 1897): 16.

"...un minois séduisant..." H. de Clarigny, *Le Mondain* (26 avril 1895); Marie, "On a giflé Mme Reillo!" *Biclous et Bidoulles*

"Elle est une lionne." *Le Véloce-Sport* (4 mars 1897): 16.

Illustration of Victorine Reillo. By the author, 2021. Source: photo by Henry R. Gibbs, "Women Cyclists at the Agricultural Hall," *The Sketch* (8 Apr. 1896): 453.

"little by little the bird builds its nest" *"Petit à petit l'oiseau fait son nid"* See Didier Loubens, *Les proverbes et locutions de la langue française, leurs origines et leur concordance avec les proverbes et locutions des autres nations* (Delagrave, 1889), 226.

"good wine, that does not need a cork!" "à bon vin il ne faut pas de bouchon" See Loubens, *Les proverbes et locutions de la langue française*, 23.

"How much are your winnings so far this season?" "Nos coureurs intimes: VII Étéogella," *Paris-Vélo* (9 octobre 1896): 1.

"...the two became inseparable." Though I suggest a romantic connection between Reillo and Étéogella, there is nothing in the research that indicates this was the case. Nevertheless, I join the two women in this way in order to introduce heroic themes into my narrative by reminding the reader of Achilles and Patroclus. See, of course, Homer's *Iliad*, but also see Gregory Nagy, "Patroklos as the Other Self of Achilles," in *The Ancient Greek Hero in 24 Hours* (Harvard UP, 2013), 146-68.

"there's no such thing as a *fête* that can't last until tomorrow" "il n'y a pas de bonne fête sans lendemain" See Loubens, *Les proverbes et locutions de la langue française*, 164.

Illustration of Gabrielle Étéogella. By the author, 2023. Source: The photo albums of Jules Beau available on Gallica.

"It was remarkably silly to get so angry over those little booklets..." I consulted numerous sources in order to better understand the potential reading habits of women of Gabrielle Étéogella's ilk: Marc Agnenot, *Le Roman populaire: recherches en paralittérature*, (Presses universitaires de Québec, 1975); Nan Enstad, *Ladies of Labor, Girls of Adventure*; Michael Denning, *Mechanic Accents: Dime Novels and Working-Class Culture in America* (Verso, 1987); Jean Tortel, "Esquisse d'un univers tragique ou le drame de la toute-puissance," *Cahiers du sud* XXIV (2e semestre 1951): 367-81.

"I have known some peace and tranquility, even if I have also known privation and hard work." Tortel, "Esquisse d'un univers tragique," 370-1.

Éponine Ollier: Reillo did not go to great lengths to conceal her true surname. However, her true given name remains a mystery. In the Official Bulletin of the *Union vélocipédique de France* for 1899, there is a record of a certain E. Ollier of Reims acquiring licence #431 with the declared pseudonym "Reillo" in "maillot et culotte noirs" (p. 732). There is no question that this is Victorine Reillo. Her real name likely was not Éponine.

Domain did indeed strike Victorine at the races and Prince Shirinskii-Shikhmatov really did send him back to Paris immediately. "Cyclisme," *Gil Blas* (mardi 2 mars 1897): 4.; "La vie sportive: cyclisme," *La Presse* (2 mars 1897): 2.;

"Le cas de Domain," *La Presse* (3 mars 1897); "Retour de Saint-Pétersbourg," *Paris-Vélo* (25 février 1897); "Un bruit fâcheux," *Paris-Vélo* (28 février 1897); Marie, "On a giflé Mme Reillo!" *Biclous et Bidoulles*, https://biclousetbidouilles.com/on-a-gifle-mme-reillo/

"The races…had nevertheless left the Russian audience bewildered and sad." "Грустные итоги: по поводу велосипедных гонок [Sad results: on the bicycle races]," *PG* (23 Feb. 1897).

"Prince Shirinskii-Shikhmatov and Colonel Gelmersen have transformed the Mikhailovskii Manège into an international cycling club." These two men did indeed organize these races: "Международные состязания велосипедистов [International Cyclist Competitions]," *PG* (4 Jan. 1897).

"The newly installed electricity…" "Велосипедные состязания в Михайловском манеже [The Bicycle Races at the Mikhailovskii Manège]," *PL* (4 (16) Jan. 1897).

"The crowds were astounding." "Международные состязания велосипедистов [International Cyclist Competitions]," *PG* (4 Jan. 1897).

Northern Palmyra: one of the many nicknames for St. Petersburg. It seems to have been especially popular with these newspapers.

"The track, with its extremely high-banked turns…" "Международные состязания велосипедистов [International Cyclist Competitions]," *PG* (4 Jan. 1897).

"In fact, Victorine had lost control and tumbled the first time the rode on it too." "Les français en Russie," *Paris-Vélo* (16 février 1897): 1.

Colonel Gelmersen and *Tant pis*: Gelmersen (or Helmersen) had a distinguished military career as a young man, serving as aide-de-camp to Grand Duke Mikhail Nikolaevich, fourth son of Nicholas I. In retirement, he became an idle troublemaker. He was known in his circles to use the French expression *tant pis* all the time: The Grand Duke Alexander of Russia, *Once a Grand Duke*. (Cassell And Company, 1932), 171.

Cavalcade of racers and two bands: "Международные состязания велосипедистов [International Cyclist Competitions]," *PG* (4 Jan. 1897); "Велосипедные состязания в Михайловском манеже [The Bicycle Races at the Mikhailovskii Manège]," *PL* (4 (16) Jan. 1897).

"…introduced a hundred-verst race into the program." "Международные состязания в Михайловском манеже [International Competitions at the Mikhailovskii Manège]," *PG* (7 Jan. 1897); "Гонка в Михайловском манеже [The Race at the Mikhailovskii Manège]," *PL* (7 (19) Jan. 1897).

"Aren't they doing themselves harm?" Many complained about the excessive physical demands cycling placed on athletes. These discussions took place in the Russian press too, right alongside the columns that lionized the races: "Вред велосипедной езды [The Harm of Bicycle Riding]," *PG* (7 Jan. 1897).

"The prince also glossed over the Luijten-Fischer six-hour race." "Международные состязания в Михайловском манеже [International Competitions at the Mikhailovskii Manège]," *PG* (13 Jan. 1897); "Матч Фишера с Лютен [The Fischer-Luijten Match]," *PL* (13 (25) Jan. 1897).

The account of the **Luijten-Fischer race** that includes the details about the amateurs' participation and the lunch break is located in "Матч Фишера с Лютеном в Михайловском манеже [The Fischer-Luijten Match at the Mikhailovskii Manège]," *RC* (16 (28) Jan. 1897): 1.

Complaints about French victories are to be found throughout the *Petersburg Gazette* and the *Petersburg Leaflet* throughout January and February 1897. See, for example, "Матчи русских и французских велосипедистов [Matches between the Russian and French Cyclists]," *PL* (17 (29) Feb. 1897).

Grand Prince Sergei Mikhailovich's prize is to be found in "Международные состязания в Михайловском манеже [International Competitions at the Mikhailovskii Manège]," *PG* (2 Feb. 1897); "Международные состязания велосипедистов [International Cyclists Races]," *PL* (2 (14) Feb. 1897).

Sextuplet: "Велосипедные состязания в Михайловском манеже [The Bicycle Races at the Mikhailovskii Manège]," *PL* (4 (16) Jan. 1897).

"...the dramatic shot-put competition held in the centre of the track." "Международные состязания велосипедистов в Михайловском манеже [International Competitions of Cyclists at the Mikhailovskii Manège]," *PG* (12 Jan. 1897).

"...the two-verst stilt-walking race between Moskvitch and Bernault..." "Международные состязания в Михайловском манеже [International Competitions at the Mikhailovskii Manège]," *PG* (17 Feb. 1897); "Матчи русских и французских велосипедистов [Matches of the Russian and French Cyclists]," *PL* (17 (29) Feb. 1897).

Lev Nikolaevich Tolstoy, the author of *Anna Karenina, War and Peace* and other notable works of fiction, was in fact in St. Petersburg in February of 1897. He was there to say farewell to Vladimir Chertkov and Pavel Biriukov, both of whom were being exiled from Russia by Tsar Nicholas II for supporting Tolstoy on the Doukhobor question. See, Ernest J. Simmons, *Leo Tolstoy, The Years of Maturity, 1880-1910* (Vintage, 1945), 227-230. Naturally, his motive for being in the capital was not publicly known. The press merely discusses seeing him. Questions about the Doukhobors and exile never come up: "Граф Л.Н. Толстой в Петербурге [Count L.N. Tolstoy in Petersburg]," *PG* (13 Feb.

1897); "Граф Л.Н. Толстой в Петербурге [Count L.N. Tolstoy in Petersburg]," *PL* (13 (25) Feb. 1897).

The race between Xidias, Zvezdochkin/Murman, and Smits: "Международные состязания в Михайловском манеже [International Competitions at the Mikhailovskii Manège]," *PG* (17 Feb. 1897).

Illustration of Murman/Zvezdochkin. By the author, 2023. Source: Collection of Rustam Bikbov.

"...a fully functional bicycle, made entirely out of paper." "Бумажный велосипед [Paper bicycle]," *PL* (7 (19) Jan. 1897).

Renaming *Paris-Vélo* into *Journal des Sports* officially occurred on 1 April 1897, though it had been announced repeatedly in the weeks leading up to that date. "Notre changement de titre," *Paris-Vélo* (mercredi 31 mars 1897): 1.

Pingault's tandem: "Электричество в роли лидера, [Electricity in the Leader's Role,]" *RC* (17 (29) Jan. 1897).

Piste de Buffalo: This was a velodrome in Paris. It was named after Buffalo Bill to commemorate his visit to Paris in 1889.

"...it is now exceeding fifty-four kilometres an hour and the battery lasts roughly an hour." "Pluie de records," *Véloce-Sport* (7 octobre 1897).

"...nor do you hold back when you've made it to the dregs": Hesiod's *Theogony*.

"At first, there was absolute silence in the manège." "Международные состязания в Михайловском манеже [International Competitions at the Mikhailovskii Manège]," *PG* (10 Feb. 1897). "Международные велосипедные состязания [International Cycling Races]," *PL* (10 (22) Feb. 1897).

Étéogella's pink outfit and ribbons: "Международные состязания в Михайловском манеже [International Competitions at the Mikhailovskii Manège]," *PG* (10 Feb. 1897). "Международные велосипедные состязания [International Cycling Races]," *PL* (10 (22) Feb. 1897).

"The first event was the one verst sprint, six laps at top speed around the track." "Международные состязания в Михайловском манеже [International Competitions at the Mikhailovskii Manège]," *PG* (10 Feb. 1897). "Международные велосипедные состязания [International Cycling Races]," *PL* (10 (22) Feb. 1897).

"Étéogella won that one too, but not without having a fight with Reillo." "Международные состязания в Михайловском манеже [International Competitions at the Mikhailovskii Manège]," *PG* (10 Feb. 1897). "Международные велосипедные состязания [International Cycling Races]," *PL* (10 (22) Feb. 1897).

"...a brisk gallop..." "Международные состязания в Михайловском манеже [International Competitions at the Mikhailovskii Manège]," *PG* (10 Feb. 1897). "Международные велосипедные состязания [International Cycling Races]," *PL* (10 (22) Feb. 1897).

"It says here that they experienced a 'fiasco' there." "Международные состязания в Михайловском манеже [International Competitions at the Mikhailovskii Manège]," *PG* (16 Feb. 1897). "Международные велосипедные состязания [International Cycling Races]," *PL* (16 (28) Feb. 1897).

"It looked like another win for pink..." "Международные состязания в Михайловском манеже [International Competitions at the Mikhailovskii Manège]," *PG* (16 Feb. 1897). "Международные состязания велосипедистов [International Cyclist Races]," *PL* (16 (28) Feb. 1897).

Fokin. "Международные состязания в Михайловском манеже [International Competitions at the Mikhailovskii Manège]," *PG* (16 Feb. 1897).

"The organizers billed the race [between the women and Fokin] as a great Russo-French match." "Международные состязания в Михайловском манеже [International Competitions at the Mikhailovskii Manège]," *PG* (22 Feb. 1897). "Международные состязания велосипедистов [International Cyclist Races]," *PL* (22 Feb. (6 Mar.) 1897).

"On the last day of racing, there had been some mixed tandem exhibition races." "Международные состязания в Михайловском манеже [International Competitions at the Mikhailovskii Manège]," *PG* (22 Feb. 1897). "Международные состязания велосипедистов [International Cyclist Races]," *PL* (22 Feb. (6 Mar.) 1897).

"The prince finally got to the part when the Styrias arrived from Austria." "Международные состязания в Михайловском манеже [International Competitions at the Mikhailovskii Manège]," *PG* (16 Feb. 1897). "Международные состязания велосипедистов [International Cyclist Races]," *PL* (16 (28) Feb. 1897); "Международные состязания в Михайловском манеже [International Competitions at the Mikhailovskii Manège]," *PG* (22 Feb. 1897). "Международные состязания велосипедистов [International Cyclist Races]," *PL* (22 Feb. (6 Mar.) 1897).

"... deep Russophile sentiment..." "Париж (от нашего корреспондента) [Paris (from our correspondent)]," *RC* (4 (16) Mar. 1897).

"The Bicycle as an Instrument of Women's Emancipation..." "Велосипед как орудие женской эмансипации [The Bicycle as an Instrument of Women's Emancipation]," *RC* 15 (20 Apr. 1896): 1; *RC* 16 (27 Apr 1896).

"...bicycles in the military...Russia's military might." France and Germany had already given serious thought to employing bicycles in military roles.

Russia was aware of this and considered introducing bicycles into its cavalry and military intelligence. See, "Боевые велосипедисты [Military Cyclists]," *PL* (1 (13) Feb. 1897).

"…just find the road that leads to the Sheremetiev's front door." On the importance of the Sheremetievs in late Imperial Russia, see Douglas Smith, *Former People: The Final Days of the Russian Aristocracy* (Farrar, Straus and Giroux, 2012), 34-42.

Peter the Great Fire Brigade: Smith, *Former People*, 35.

"…the first time he ever saw bicycles was when he visited…the Late Alexander II…" Igor Zimin, Взрослый мир императорских резиденций. Повседневная жизнь российского императорского двора. [*The Adult World of the Imperial Residences. Everyday Life in the Russian Imperial Court.*] (Tsentropoligraf, 2010), 192.

Nikolai Vasilievich Kleigels: I use the title "mayor" to aid in storytelling, but Imperial Russia did not have elected municipal representatives. Kleigels's true title was gradonachal'nik or "city administrator."

"…the enormous task of increasing St. Petersburg's electrical supply." Jonathan Coopersmith, "Electrification, 1886-1914," *The Electrification of Russia, 1880-1926.* (Cornell UP, 1992).

"…bumping into each other on the streets at night… [etc.]" "Вопрос об освещении Петербурга [The Question of Lighting Petersburg]," *PG* (5 Feb. 1897).

"…Rozhdestvennyi District was being deprived of electricity…" "В думе (заседание 5-го марта) [In the Duma (Session of 5th March)]" *PL* (6 (18) Mar. 1897).

"The closest waterfall was at Imrata along the Vuoksi River." Timo Myllyntaus, "Electrical Imperialism or Multinational Cooperation? The Role of Big Business in Supplying Light and Power to St. Petersburg before 1917," *Business and Economic History* 26:2 (Winter 1997): 540-9.

"…the need for heavy French investment." René Girault, "Emprunts russes et investissements français en Russie," *Le mouvement social* 80 (juillet-septembre 1972): 49-58.

Illustration of Exterior of the Mikhailovskii Manège. By the author, 2023.

Illustration of a Clown from the Ciniselli Circus. By the author, 2023. Source: "L'Olympia," *Véloce-Sport* (1 avr. 1897).

Andrei Alexandrovich Shirinskii-Shikhmatov, older brother of Dmitri Alexandrovich. He collected icons, led a distinguished career in the Ministry of Internal Affairs and later became the Governor of Saratov Gubernia from

1913-1915. In 1915, he was promoted to Member of Council with the Ministry of Internal Affairs.

"...peasants in Poland..." Goremykin had his ministry writing about the Polish peasants, again, as he had already done once under Alexander II. Альманах современных русских государственных деятелей. [*The Almanac of Contemporary Russian State Agents.*] (St. Petersburg: Isadore Gol'dberg, 1897), 147-9.

"...trampled to death..." At Tsar Nicholas II's coronation in Moscow there was a pedestrian stampede at the Khodynka field.

CHAPTER FOUR: TESSIE REYNOLDS

Tessie Reynolds. Sheila Hanlon, "Tessie Reynolds: The Stormy Petrel in the Struggle for Women's Equality in Cycle Racing and Dress," *Women's Cycling* (27 May 2018); Hannah Ross, *Revolutions*, 51-4; Kat Jungnickel, *Bikes and Bloomers*, 73-5; 127.

"Every wheelman who has managed to maintain a belief..." Hanlon, "Tessie Reynolds," *Women's Cycling* (27 May 2018).

"...Miss Reynolds has accomplished more in three weeks in stirring up opinion about ladies' rational dress..." Jungnickel, *Bikes and Bloomers*, 127.

Illustration of Tessie Reynolds. By the author, 2021. Source: Brighton and Hove Museums.

ACKNOWLEDGEMENTS

This book has benefitted from the support of numerous individuals and resources.

First, I wish to acknowledge three teachers who served as role-models and sources of encouragement in my life. Anthony Dayton, my high school teacher, encouraged me unstintingly during my first steps at writing. Janine Langan, my favourite undergraduate professor, showed me that literature is a vast repository of humanity's abundant enthusiasm and curiosity, built for our enjoyment. DTO showed me that literature can be a vocation, if you want it to be. Its bellows are contemplation, discipline, thoroughness and, most of all, patience.

Next, I wish to acknowledge the family and friends who helped read earlier drafts of this project. Special mention goes out to Holly Wilson, Agnieszka Polakowska, Pamela Humpage, Reta Ormond, Paul Belyea, the tireless Phillip Holland and my very old and dear writing friend, Chris Gallagher. The staff at Velotique, my local bike shop, also read early drafts: thank you, Spencer Tyber, Tommy Lee, Rob Bartel and John Gibson. I shared early versions of parts of this book at David Bester's *Start Writing* group and benefited greatly from the feedback and support I received there, not only from David, but also from Alexis Silverman, Angelica LeMinh and David Bosworth. I also thank Berit Langmoen Dullerud for teaching me about Scandinavian folklore and introducing me to Asbjørnsen and Moe. Madison Shymberg managed the helm through the publishing process with Friesen Press. I appreciated her kind and knowledgeable guidance through all stages of this book's production.

A book like this cannot be done without standing on the shoulders of the incredible work of other researchers. It is not possible to mention all the works I referred to here, but some authors and works do deserve special mention: Kat Jungnickel's *Bikes and Bloomers* (2018), Roger Gilles's *Women on the Move* (2018), Hannah Ross's *Revolutions* (2020), as well as the websites of Sheila Hanlon (*Women's Cycling*), and Mike Fishpool (*Playing Pasts*). I also wish to thank Philip Gordon Mackintosh of Brock University for generously sharing his research about bicycling women in the bourgeoisie.

It is equally important to acknowledge the incredible generosity of the numerous research resources I used while preparing this project. The Toronto Public Library has proven to be a faithful and generous ally at all stages of research. I am particularly grateful to its Interlibrary Loan service and the Canadian universities who shared their collections with me under its auspices. Numerous online resources were indispensable: Hathi Digital Trust, the Digital Newspaper Hub of the Minnesota Historical Society, the Gallica Online Collection of the Bibliothèque nationale de France, and the newspaper archive at the Russian National Library, St. Petersburg Branch. Special mention must go to Alice Roepke, the great niece of Tillie Anderson, who permitted me to make an original illustration using her photo archive for reference. (Check it out: http://tillieanderson.com/tillie/)

As a stay-at-home dad, I would be remiss if I did not acknowledge the wonderful support of my mother, my lovely wife, and my daughters. I hope these stories inspire you. After all, they are dedicated to you. I also wish to acknowledge my late father, Richard Sinclair Ormond. I used many of your tools and lessons when I made the illustrations for this book.

Lastly, I wish to acknowledge and thank Lisette, Tillie, Victorine, Gabrielle, Tessie and all the other women who appear in these stories. You lived remarkable lives, and though I have certainly taken great liberties with some of the finer details, I have accurately preserved, to the best of my ability, the broader strokes of your participation in the events here recorded. I hope that I have caught at least some of the truth about your lives and about women's bicycle racing in the 1890s.